LORNA DOONE

A ROMANCE OF EXMOOR

R. D. BLACKMORE

CONTENTS

1

A SUDDEN END TO SCHOOL LIFE

If anybody cares to read a simple tale told simply, I, John Ridd, of the parish of Oare, in the county of Somerset, yeoman and churchwarden, have seen and had a share in some doings of this neighbourhood, which I will try to set down in order, God sparing my life and memory. I write for the clearing of our parish from ill-fame, though I am nothing more than a plain unlettered man, not read in foreign languages, as a gentleman might be, nor gifted with long words (even in mine own tongue), save what I have won from the Bible, or Master William Shakespeare, whom, in the face of common opinion, I do value highly. In short, I am an ignoramus, but pretty well for a yeoman.

My father being of good substance, at least as we reckon in Exmoor, and owning, from many generations, one, and that the best and largest, of the three farms into which our parish is divided, he, John Ridd, the elder, churchwarden and overseer, being a great admirer of learning, and well able to write his name, sent me his only son to be schooled at Tiverton, in the county of Devon. For the chief boast of that ancient town next to its woollen-staple is a worthy grammar-school, the largest in the west of England, founded and handsomely endowed in the year 1604, by Master Peter Blundell, of the same place, clothier. Here, by the time I was twelve years old, I had risen into the upper school; but it came to pass, by the grace of God, that I was called away from learning, while sitting at the desk of the junior first in the upper school, and beginning the Greek verb.

On the 29th day of November, in the year of our Lord 1673, the very day when I was twelve years old, and had spent all my substance in sweetmeats, I was standing on the gate of the school with some of the boys, and we were hoping to see a good string of pack-horses come by, with troopers to protect them. For the day-boys had brought us word that some intending their way to the town had lain that morning at Sampford Peveril, and must be in ere nightfall, because Mr. Faggus was after them. Now Mr. Faggus was my first cousin, and an honour to the family, being a North-molton man, of great renown on the highway, from Barum town even to London. Therefore, of course, I hoped that he would catch the packmen, and the boys were asking my opinion, as of an oracle, about it.

A certain boy leaning up against me would not allow my elbow room, and struck me very sadly in the stomach part. And this I felt so unkindly, that I smote him straightway in the face without tarrying to consider it, or weighing the question. It was therefore settled for us that we should move to the " Ironing-box ", as the triangle of turf is called, where the two causeways coming from the school-porch and the hall-porch meet, and our fights are mainly celebrated; only we must wait until the convoy of horses had passed, and then make a ring by candlelight, and the other boys would like it. But suddenly there came round the post where the letters of our founder are, not from the way of Taunton, but from the side of Lowman bridge, a very small string of horses, only two indeed (counting for one the pony), and a red-faced man on the bigger nag.

" Plaise ye, worshipful masters," he said, being feared of the gateway, " carn 'e tull whur our Jan Ridd be ? "

" Hyur a be, ees fai, Jan Ridd," answered a sharp little chap, making game of John Fry's language.

" Zhow un up, then," says John Fry, poking his

whip through the bars at us; "zhow un up, and putt un aowt."

The other little chaps pointed at me, but some began to holla; but I knew what I was about.

"Oh, John, John," I cried; "what's the use of your coming now, and my pony Peggy over the moors too, and it is so cruel cold for her? The holidays don't begin till Wednesday fortnight, John. To think of your not knowing that!"

John Fry leaned forward in the saddle, and turned his eyes away from me; and then there was a noise in his throat, like a snail crawling on a window-pane.

"Oh, us knaws that wull enough, Maister Jan; reckon every Oare man knaw that, without go to skoo-ull, like you doth. Your moother have kep arl the apples up, and old Betty toorned the black puddens, and none dare set trap for a blag-bird. Arl for thee, lad; every bit of it now for thee!"

He checked himself suddenly and frightened me. I knew that John Fry's way so well.

"And father, and father—oh, how is father?" I pushed the boys right and left as I said it. "John, is father up in town? He always used to come for me, and leave nobody else to do it."

"Vayther coodn't lave 'ouze by raison of the Christmas bakkon comin' on, and zome of the cider welted."

He looked at the nag's ears as he said it; and being up to John Fry's ways, I knew that it was a lie and my heart fell, like a lump of lead. But whatever lives or dies, business must be attended to.

"Come up, Jack," remembered one of the boys, lifting me under the chin, "he hit you, and you hit him, you know."

"Pay your debts before you go," said a monitor, striding up to me, after hearing how the honour lay; "Ridd, you must go through with it."

I now felt upon me a certain responsibility, a dutiful need to maintain in the presence of John Fry the manliness of the Ridd family and the honour of Exmoor. Hitherto none had

worsted me, although in the three years of my schooling
I had fought more than three-score battles, and bedewed
with blood every plant of grass towards the middle of the
Ironing-box. And this success I owed at first to no skill of my
own, until I came to know better; for up to twenty or thirty
fights, I struck as nature guided me, no wiser than a father-
long-legs in the heat of a lanthorn; but I had conquered,
partly through my native strength and the Exmoor toughness
in me, and still more that I could not see when I had gotten
my bellyfull. But now I was like to have that and more, for
my heart was down to begin with; and then Robert Snell was
a bigger boy than I had ever encountered, and as thick in the
skull and hard in the brain as even I could claim to be.

For a time I had but little hope; my chest was pumping
hard and I had a great desire to fall away. Then John Fry says
in my ears, as if he were clapping spurs into a horse.

" Never thee knack under, Jan, or never coom naigh
Hexmoor no more."

With that it was all up with me. A simmering buzzed in
my heavy brain, and a light came through my eye-places.
At once I set both fists again, and my heart stuck to me like
cobbler's wax. Robin let at me with his left hand, and I
gave him my right between his eyes, and he blinked, and
was not pleased with it. I feared him not, and spared him
not, neither spared myself. My breath came again, and my
heart stood cool, and my eyes struck fire no longer. Only I
knew that I would die, sooner than shame my birthplace.
How the rest of it was I know not; only that I had the end of
it, and helped to put Robin in bed.

John Fry and I left the town of the two fords, which they
say is the meaning of Tiverton, very early in the morning,
after lying one day to rest, as was demanded by the nags,
sore of foot and foundered. For my part, too, I was glad to
rest, having aches all over me, and very heavy bruises; and
we lodged at the sign of the White Horse Inn, in the street
called Gold Street. Though still John Fry was dry with me
of the reason of his coming, and only told lies about father,

and could not keep them agreeable, I hoped for the best, as all boys will, especially after a victory. And I thought perhaps father had sent for me, because he had a good harvest, and rats were bad in the corn chamber.

It was high noon before we got to Dulverton that day, near to which town the river Exe and its big brother Barle have union. My mother had an uncle living there, but we were not to visit his house this time, at which I was somewhat astonished, since we needs must stop for at least two hours, to bait our horses thorough well, before coming to the black bogway. The bogs are very good in frost, except where the hot springs rise; but as yet there had been no real frost this year.

The road from Bampton to Dulverton had not been very delicate, yet nothing to complain of much—no deeper, indeed, than the hocks of a horse, except in the rotten places. The day was inclined to be mild and foggy, and both nags sweated freely; but Peggy carrying little weight (for my wardrobe was upon Smiler, and John Fry grumbling always), we could easily keep in front.

John had been rather bitter with me, but now, at Dulverton, we dined upon the rarest and choicest victuals that ever I did taste. Even now, at my time of life, to think of it gives me appetite.

When the meal was done, and Peggy and Smiler had dined well also, out I went to wash at the pump, being a lover of soap and water, at all risk, except of my dinner. And John Fry, who cared very little to wash, save Sabbath days in his own soap, and who had kept me from the pump by threatening loss of the meal, out he came in a satisfied manner, with a piece of quill in his hand, to lean against a doorpost and listen to the horses feeding, and have his teeth ready for supper.

Then a lady's-maid came out, and the sun was on her face. With a long Italian glass in her fingers very daintily, she came up to the pump in the middle of the yard, where I was running the water off all my head and shoulders, and arms, and some of my breast even, and though I had glimpsed her through the sprinkle, it gave me quite a turn to see her, child as I was, in my open aspect. But she looked at me, no whit abashed, and said to me in a brazen manner, as if I had been nobody, while I was shrinking behind the pump and craving to get my shirt on—" Good leetle boy, come hither to me. Fine heaven! How blue your eyes are, and your skin like snow; but some naughty man has beaten it black. Oh, leetle boy, let me feel it. Ah, how it must have hurt you! "

All this time she was touching my breast, here and there, very lightly, with her delicate brown fingers, and I understood from her voice and manner that she was not of this country, but a foreigner. And then I was not so shy of her, because I could talk better English than she; and yet I longed for my jerkin, but liked not to be rude to her.

" If you please, madam, I must go. John Fry is waiting by the tapster's door, and Peggy neighing to me. If you please, we must get home tonight; and father will be waiting for me this side of the telling house."

" There, there, you shall go, leetle dear, and perhaps I will go after you. Now make the pump flow, my dear, and give me the good water."

I pumped for her very heartily, then she made a courtesy to me and wanted to kiss me; but I ducked under the pump handle, and she knocked her chin on the knob of it; and the hostlers came out, and asked whether they would do as well.

Upon this she retreated up the yard, with a certain dark dignity, and a foreign way of walking, which stopped them at once from going farther, because it was so different from the fashion of their sweethearts.

Now, up to the end of Dulverton town, on the northward side of it, where the two new pig-sties be, the Oare folk and the Watchett folk must trudge on together, until we come to a broken cross, where a murdered man lies buried. Peggy and Smiler went up the hill, as if nothing could be too much for them after the beans they had eaten, and suddenly turning a corner of trees, we happened upon a great coach and six horses labouring very heavily. John Fry rode on with his hat in his hand, as became him towards the quality, but I was amazed to that degree that I left my cap on my head, and drew bridle without knowing it.

For in the front seat of the coach, which was half-way open, being of new city make and the day in want of air, sate the foreign lady, who had met me at the pump and offered to salute me. By her side was a little girl, dark-haired and very wonderful, with a wealthy softness on her, as if she must have her own way. I could not look at her for two glances, and she did not look at me for one, being such a little child, and busy with the hedges. But in the honourable place sate a handsome lady, very warmly dressed, and sweetly delicate of colour. And close to her was a lively child, two or it may be three years old, bearing a white cockade in his hat, and staring at all and everybody. Now he saw Peggy, and took such a liking to her, that the lady his mother—if so she were—was forced to look at my pony and me. And she looked at us very kindly, and with a sweetness rarely found in the women who milk the cows for us.

Then I took off my cap to the beautiful lady, without asking wherefore; and she put up her hand and kissed it to me, thinking, perhaps, that I looked like a gentle and good little boy; for folk always call me innocent, though God knows I never was that. But now the foreign lady, or lady's-maid, as it might be, who had been busy with litt dark-eyes, turned upon all this going on, and looked me straight in the face. I was about to salute her but, strange to say, she stared at my eyes as if she had never seen me before, neither wished to see me again. At this I was so startled, such things being out of my knowledge, that I startled Peggy also with the muscle of my legs, and she being fresh from stable, and the mire scraped off with cask-hoop, broke away so suddenly that I could do no more than turn round and lower my cap, now five months old, to the beautiful lady. Soon I overtook John Fry, and asked him all about them, and how it was we had missed their starting from the hostel. But John would never talk much until after a gallon of cider; and all that I could win out of him was that they were " murdering Papishers ", and little he cared to do with them, or the devil as they came from.

We saw no more of them after that, but turned into the sideway, and soon had the fill of our hands and eyes to look to our own going. For the road got worse and worse, until there was none at all. But we pushed on as best we might, with doubt of reaching home any time, except by special grace of God.

The fog came down upon the moors as thick as I ever saw it, and there was no sound of any sort, nor a breath of wind to guide us, but John jogged on into the homeward tract, unerring. We did not reach home without incident, however.

" Harken, lad! Harken!" John Fry said on a sudden. " Us be naigh the Doone-track now, two maile from Dunkery Beacon Hill, the haighest place of Hexmoor. So happen they be abroad tonight, us must crawl on our belly-places, boy."

I knew at once what he meant—those bloody Doones of Bagworthy, the awe of all Devon and Somerset, outlaws, traitors, murderers. My little legs began to tremble to and fro upon Peggy's sides.

" But John," I whispered warily, sidling close to his saddle-bow, " dear John, you don't think they will see us in such a fog as this ? "

" Never God made vog as could stop their eyesen," he whispered in answer, fearfully; " here us be by the hollow ground. Zober, lad, goo zober now, if thee wish to see thy moother."

We were come to a long deep " goyal ", as they call it on Exmoor, a long trough among wild hills, falling towards the plain country.

We rode very carefully down our side, and through the soft grass at the bottom, and all the while we listened as if the air was a speaking trumpet. Then gladly we breasted our nags to the rise, and were coming to the comb of it, when I heard something, and caught John's arm, and he bent his hand to the shape of his ear. It was the sound of horses' feet, knocking up through splashy ground, as if the bottom sucked them. Then a grunting of weary men, and the lifting noise of stirrups, and sometimes the clank of iron mixed with the wheezy croning of leather, and the blowing of hairy nostrils.

" God's sake, Jack, slip round her belly, and let her go where she wull."

As John Fry whispered, so I did, for he was off Smiler by this time; but our two pads were too fagged to go far, and began to nose about and crop, sniffing more than they needed have done. I crept to John's side very softly, with the bridle on my arm.

" Let goo braidle; let goo, lad. Plaise God they take them for forest-ponies, or they'll zend a bullet through us."

Then just as the foremost horseman passed, scarce twenty yards below us, a puff of wind came up the glen, and the fog rolled off before it. And suddenly a strong red light, cast by the cloud-weight downwards, spread like fingers over the moorland, opened the alleys of darkness, and hung on the steel of the riders. Heavy men and large of stature, reckless how they bore their guns, or how they sate their horses, with leathern jerkins, and long boots, and iron plates on breast and head, plunder heaped behind their saddles, and flagons slung in front of them; more than thirty went along, like clouds upon red sunset. Some had carcases of sheep swinging with their skins on, others had deer and one even had a child flung across his saddle-bow.

It touched me so to see that child, a prey among those vultures, that in my foolish rage and burning I stood up and shouted to them, leaping on a rock, and raving out of all possession. Two of them turned round, and one set his carbine at me, but the other said it was but a pixie, and bade him keep his powder. Little they knew, and less thought I,

17

that the pixie then before them would dance their castle down one day.

" Small thanks to thee, Jan," cried John Fry, "·as my new waife bain't a widder. And who be you to zupport of her, and her son, if she have one ? Zarve thee right, if I was to chuck thee down into the Doone-track. Zim thee'll come to un, zooner or later, if this be the zample of thee."

And that was all he had to say, instead of thanking God! For if ever born man was in a fright, and ready to thank God for anything, the name of that man was " John Fry ", not more than five minutes agone.

Eventually we reached home, Plover's Barrows Farm, but my father never came to meet us and all at once my heart went down, and all my breast was hollow.

But by and by a noise came down, as of woman's weeping; and there my mother and sister were, choking and holding together. Although they were my dearest loves, I could not bear to look at them, until they seemed to want my help, and turned away, that I might come.

2

A RASH VISIT

My dear father had been killed by the Doones of Bagworthy, while riding home from Porlock market, on the Saturday evening. With him were six brother-farmers, all of them very sober.

These seven farmers were jogging along, helping one and another in the troubles of the road, and singing goodly hymns and songs to keep their courage moving, when suddenly a horseman stopped in the starlight full across them.

By dress and arms and by his size and stature, they knew him to be a Doone. Six of them pulled out their horses, but my father rode at the Doone robber who dodged him and turned to plundering the others. Then concealed men sprang up and attacked him whom he beat off. Beyond the range of his staff a man was crouching by the peatstack, with a long gun set to his shoulder, and he got poor father against the sky, and I cannot tell the rest of it. Only they knew that Smiler came home, with blood upon his withers, and father was found in the morning dead on the moor, with his ivy-twisted cudgel lying broken under him.

It was more of woe than wonder, being such days of violence, that mother knew herself a widow, and her children fatherless. Of children there were only three, none of us fit to be useful yet, only to comfort mother, by making her to work for us. I, John Ridd, was the eldest, and felt it a heavy thing on me; next came sister Annie, with about two years between us; and then the little Eliza.

Now, before I got home and found my sad loss—and no boy ever loved his father better than I loved mine—mother had done a most wondrous thing, which made all the neighbours say she must be mad, at least. Upon the Monday morning, while her husband lay unburied, she cast a white hood over her hair, and gathered a black cloak around her, and taking counsel of no one, set off on foot for the Doone-gate.

In the early afternoon she came to the hollow and barren entrance; where in truth there was no gate, only darkness to go through. If I get on with this story I shall have to tell of it by and by, as I saw it afterwards; and will not dwell there now. Enough that no gun was fired at her, only her eyes were covered over, and somebody led her by the hand, with no wish to hurt her.

A very rough and headstrong road was all that she remembered, for she could not think as she wished to do, with the cold iron pushed against her. At the end of this road they delivered her eyes and she could scarce believe them.

For she stood at the head of a deep, green valley, carved from out the mountains in a perfect oval, with a fence of sheer rock standing round it, eighty feet or a hundred high; from whose brink black wooded hills swept up to the skyline. By her side a little river glided out from underground with a soft dark babble, unawares of daylight; then growing brighter, lapsed away and fell into the valley. Farther down, on either bank, were covered houses, fourteen of them, built of stone, square and roughly cornered, set as if the brook were meant to be the street between them. Only one room high they were, and not placed opposite each other, but in and out as skittles are; only that the first of all, which proved to be the captain's, was a sort of double house, or rather two joined together by a plank-bridge over the river.

Two men led my mother down a steep and gliddery stair-way, like the ladder of a hay-mow; and thence, from the break of the falling water, as far as the house of the captain. And there at the door they left her trembling, strung as she was to speak her mind.

A tall old man, Sir Ensor Doone, came out with a bill-hook in his hand, and hedgers' gloves going up his arms, as if he were no better than a labourer at ditch-work. Only in his mouth and eyes, his gait, and most of all his voice, even a child could know and feel, that here was no ditch-labourer.

" Good woman, you are none of us. Who has brought you hither ? "

" What you mean, I know not. Traitors! Cut-throats! Cowards! I am here to ask for my husband."

And by the way she cried, he knew that they had killed her husband. Then, having felt of grief himself, he was not angry with her, but left her to begin again.

" Loth would I be," said mother, sobbing with her new red handkerchief, and looking at the pattern of it, " loth indeed, Sir Ensor Doone, to accuse anyone unfairly. But I have lost the very best husband God ever gave to a woman and I knew him when he was to your belt, and I not up to your knee, sir; and never an unkind word he spoke, nor stopped me short in speaking."

" This matter must be seen to; it shall be seen to at once," the old man answered, moved a little in spite of all his knowledge. " Madam, if any wrong has been done, trust the honour of a Doone; I will redress it to my utmost. Come inside and rest yourself, while I ask about it. What was your good husband's name, and when and where fell this mishap?"

"Deary me," said mother, as he sat a chair for her very polite, but she would not sit upon it; "Saturday morning I was a wife, sir; and Saturday night I was a widow, and my children are fatherless. My husband's name was John Ridd, sir, as everyone knows; and there was not a finer or better man in Somerset or Devon."

"Madam, this is a serious thing," Sir Ensor Doone said graciously and showing grave concern. "My boys are a little wild I know; and yet I cannot think that they would willingly harm anyone. And yet—and yet, you do look sad. Send Counsellor to me," he shouted from the door of his house; and down the valley went the call, "Send Counsellor to Captain."

Counsellor Doone came in. A square-built man of enormous strength, but a foot below the Doone stature (which I shall describe hereafter), he carried a long grey beard descending to the leather of his belt. Great eyebrows overhung his face, like ivy on a pollard oak, and under them two large brown eyes, as of an owl when muting. And he had a power of hiding his eyes, or showing them bright, like a blazing fire. He stood there with his beaver off, and mother tried to look at him; but he seemed not to descry her.

"Counsellor," said Sir Ensor Doone, standing back in his height from him, "here is a lady of good repute in this part of the country, who charges the Doones with having unjustly slain her husband. . . ."

"Murdered him! Murdered him!" cried my mother.

The square man with the long grey beard, quite unmoved by anything, drew back to the door, and spoke, and his voice was like a fall of stones in the bottom of a mine.

"Few words will be enow for this. Four or five of our best-behaved and most peaceful gentlemen went to the little market of Porlock with a lump of money. They bought some household stores and comforts at a very high price, and pricked upon the homeward road, away from vulgar revellers. When they drew bridle to rest their horses, in the shelter of a peat-rick, the night being dark and sudden, a robber of great size and strength rode into the midst of them, thinking to kill or terrify. His arrogance, and hardihood, at first amazed them, but they would not give up without a blow goods which were on trust with them. He had smitten three of them senseless, for the power of his arm was terrible, whereupon the last man tried to ward his blow with a pistol. Carver, sir, it was, our brave and noble Carver, who saved the lives of his brethren and his own; and glad enow they were to escape. Notwithstanding, we hoped it might be only a flesh-wound and not to speed him in his sins."

As this atrocious tale of lies turned up joint by joint before her, mother was too much amazed to do any more than look at him, as if the earth must open; then she dried her tears in haste and went into the cold air, for fear of speaking mischief.

But when she was on the homeward road, and the sentinels had charge of her, blinding her eyes, as if she were not blind enough with weeping, some one came in haste behind her, and thrust a heavy leathern bag into the limp weight of her hand.

" Captain sends you this," he whispered; " take it to the little ones."

But mother let it fall in a heap, as if it had been a blind worm; and then for the first time crouched before God, that even the Doones should pity her.

* * * * *

Good folk may wonder how these lawless Doones came to dwell in our lawful land. It all goes back to the troublous year 1640 when, amid the great estates in the north country that were suddenly confiscated, was that one held in joint ownership by Sir Ensor Doone and his cousin, the Earl of Lorne and Dykemont. Though divided from his estate Lord Lorne still remained well-to-do, but Sir Ensor was left a beggar and—rightly or wrongly—blamed his cousin for his impoverishment. Some say that in the bitterness of that wrong and outrage he committed murder or some violent deed. Be that as it may, he was indeed made a felon outlaw and in great despair resolved to settle in an outlandish part. An evil day it was for us when he chose the west of England. Here in an inaccessible valley the Doones multiplied and sustained themselves by robbery, rapine and murder that soon led to their becoming the terror of the countryside. Yet so strongly had they entrenched themselves in Doone valley that none dared assault their stronghold or risk the vengeance of these hated intruders, and we Ridds were no bolder than the rest when they struck down my dear father. Fearing further ado, we could do naught but bury him quietly in the sloping little churchyard of Oare.

3

A BOY AND A GIRL

During those winter days I fetched down father's gun and after long practice became quite proficient at its use.

Many a winter night went by in a hopeful and pleasant manner, with the hissing of the bright round bullets, cast into the water, and the spluttering of the great red apples, which Annie was roasting for me.

Almost everybody knows, in our part of the world at least, how pleasant and soft the fall of the land is about Plover's Barrows Farm. All above it is strong dark mountain, spread with heath, and desolate, but near our house the valleys cove, and open warmth and shelter. But all below, where the valley ends and the Lynn stream goes along with it, pretty meadows slope their breast, and the sun spreads on the water. And nearly all this is ours, till you come to Nicholas Snowe's land. But about two miles below our farm, the Bagworthy water runs into the Lynn, and makes a real river of it. Thence it hurries away, with strength, and a force of wilful waters, under the foot of a bare-faced hill, and so to rocks and woods again, where the stream is covered over, and dark, heavy pools delay it. Neither Annie or I had been up the Bagworthy water, which ran out of the Doone valley, a mile or so from the mouth of it.

But when I was turned fourteen years old, and put into good small-clothes, buckled at the knee, and strong blue worsted hosen, knitted by my mother, it happened to me without choice, I may say, to explore the Bagworthy water. And it came about in this wise.

My mother had long been ailing, and not well able to eat much. Now I chanced to remember, that mother was very fond of loaches. So I now resolved to get some loaches for her, to make her eat a bit.

I set forth without a word to anyone, in the forenoon of St. Valentine's Day, 1676. Snow lay here and there in patches in the hollow of the banks.

When I had travelled two miles or so, conquered now and then with cold, and coming out to rub my legs with a lively friction, and only fishing here and there because of the tumbling water; suddenly, in an open space, where meadows spread about it, I found a good stream flowing softly into the body of our brook. And it brought, so far as I could guess by the sweep of it under my kneecaps, a larger power of clear water than the Lynn itself had; only it came more quietly down, not being troubled with stairs and steps but gliding smoothly and forcibly, as if upon some set purpose.

Now all the turn of all my life hung upon that moment. It seemed a sad business to go back now and tell Annie there were no loaches; and yet it was a frightful thing, knowing what I did of it, to venture, where no grown man durst, up the Bagworthy water.

However, as I ate more and more of Betty Muxworthy's sweet brown bread my spirit arose within me. So I went stoutly up under the branches which hung so dark on the Bagworthy river.

I had very comely sport of loaches, trout and minnows, forking some and tickling some, and driving others to shallow nooks, whence I could bail them ashore. Now, if you have ever been fishing you will not wonder that I was

led on, forgetting all about danger, and taking no heed of
the time. For now the day was falling fast behind the brown
of the hill-tops; and the trees being void of leaf and hard,
seemed giants ready to beat me. And every moment as the
sky was clearing up for a white frost, the cold of the water
got worse and worse, until I was fit to cry with it. And so
in a sorry plight, I came to an opening in the bushes, where
a great black pool lay in front of me, whitened with snow
(as I thought) at the sides, till I saw it was only foam-froth.

Now, though I could swim with great ease and comfort,
and feared no depth of water, when I could fairly come to it,
yet I had no desire to go head over ears into this great pool.
But soon I saw the reason of the stir and depth of that great
pit, as well as of the roaring sound which long had made me
wonder. For skirting round one side, I came to the foot of a
long pale slide of water, coming smoothly to me, without any
break or hindrance, for a hundred yards or more, and
fenced on either side with cliff, sheer, straight and shining.
Although greatly scared I was very curious.

I bestowed my fish around my neck more tightly, and not
stopping to look much for fear of fear, crawled along over
the fork of rocks, where the water had scooped the stone out;
and shunning thus the ledge from whence it rose, softly I
let my feet into the dip and rush of the torrent.

And here I had reckoned without my host, although (as
I thought) so clever; and it was much but that I went down
into the great black pool, and had never been heard of more;
and this must have been the end of me except for my trusty
loach-fork. I grasped the good loach-stick under a knot,
and steadied me with my left hand, and so with a sigh of
despair began my course up the fearful torrent-way. To me
it seemed half a mile at least of sliding water above me, but
in truth it was little more than a furlong, as I came to know
afterwards.

The water was only six inches deep, or from that to nine
at the utmost, and all the way up I could see my feet looking
white in the gloom of the hollow, and here and there I

found resting-place to hold on by the cliff and pant awhile And gradually as I went on a warmth of courage breathed in me to think that perhaps no other had dared to try that pass before me.

Only I must acknowledge that the greatest danger of all was just where I saw no jeopardy, but ran up a patch of black ooze-weed in a very boastful manner, being now not far from the summit. Here I fell very piteously, and was like to have broken my knee-cap, and the torrent got hold of my other leg, while I was indulging the bruised one. In dreadful fright, I laboured hard with both legs and arms going like a mill. At last the light was coming upon me, and again I fought towards it; then suddenly I felt fresh air, and fell into it headlong.

When I came to myself again, a little girl kneeling at my side was rubbing my forehead tenderly, with a dock-leaf and a handkerchief.

" Oh, I am so glad " she whispered softly, as I opened my eyes and looked at her; " now you will try to be better, won't you ? "

I had never heard so sweet a sound as came from between her bright red lips, while there she knelt and gazed at me; neither had I ever seen anything so beautiful as the large, dark eyes intent upon me, full of pity and wonder.

" What is your name ? " she said, as if she had every right to ask me; " and how did you come here, and what are these wet things in this great bag ? "

" You had better let them alone," I said; " they are loaches for my mother. But I will give you some, if you like. But how you are looking at me! I never saw anyone like you before. My name is John Ridd. What is your name ? "

" Lorna Doone," she answered in a low voice, as if afraid of it and hanging her head, so that I could only see her forehead and eye-lashes; " if you please, my name is Lorna Doone; and I thought you must have known it."

Then I stood up and touched her hand, and tried to make her look at me, but she only turned away guiltily.

"Don't cry," I said, "whatever you do. I am sure you have never done any harm. I will give you all my fish, Lorna, and catch some more for mother; only don't be angry with me."

She flung her little soft arms up, in the passion of her tears, and looked at me so piteously, that what did I do but kiss her. It seemed to be a very odd thing, when I came to think of it, because I hated kissing so, as all honest boys must do. But she touched my heart with a sudden delight, like a cowslip blossom (though there were none to be seen yet) and the sweetest flowers of spring.

Now, seeing how I heeded her, and feeling that I had kissed her, although she was such a little girl, eight years old or thereabouts, she turned to the stream in a bashful manner, and began to watch the water, and rubbed one leg against the other.

I for my part, being vexed at her behaviour to me, took up all my things to go, and made a fuss about it; to let her know I was going. But she did not call me back at all, as I had made sure she would do; moreover, I knew that to try the descent was almost certain death to me, and it looked as dark as pitch; so at the mouth I turned round again and came back to her, and said, "Lorna."

"Oh, I thought you were gone," she answered. "Why did you ever come here? Do you know what they would do to us, if they found you here with me?"

"Beat us, I dare say, very hard, or me at least. They could never beat you."

"N^. They would kill us both outright, and bury us here by the water; and the water often tells me I must come to that."

"But what should they kill me for?"

"Because you have found the way up here, and they never could believe it. Now, please to go; oh, please to go. They will kill us both in a moment. Yes, I like you very much"— for I was teasing her to say it—"very much indeed, and I will call you John Ridd, if you like; only please to go, John.

27

And when your feet are well, you know, you can come and tell me how they are—hush! "

A shout came down from the valley; and all my heart was trembling like water after sunset, and Lorna's face was altered from pleasant play to terror. She shrank to me and looked up at me, with such a power of weakness, that I at once made up my mind, to save her, or to die with her. A tingle went through all my bones, and I only longed for my carbine. The little girl took courage from me, and put her cheek quite close to mine.

" Come with me down the waterfall. I can carry you easily; and mother will take care of you."

" No, no," she cried, as I took her up: " I will tell you what to do. They are only looking for me. You see that hole, that hole there ? "

She pointed to a little niche in the rock which verged the meadow, about fifty yards away from us. In the fading of the twilight I could just descry it.

" Yes, I see it; but they will see me crossing the grass to get there."

" Look! Look! " she could hardly speak. " There is a way out from the top of it; they would kill me if I told it. Oh, here they come! I can see them."

But I drew her behind the withy bushes and close down to the water, where it was quiet and shelving deep, ere it came to the lip of the chasm. Here they might not see either of us from the upper valley.

Crouching in that hollow nest, as children get together in ever so little compass, I saw a dozen fierce men come down, on the other side of the water, not bearing any fire-arms, but looking lax and jovial, as if they were come from riding and a dinner taken hungrily. " Queen queen! " they were shouting, here and there, and now and then: " where the pest is our little queen gone ? "

" They always call me queen, and I am to be queen by and by," Lorna whispered to me, with her soft cheek on my rough one, and her little heart beating against me. " Oh, they are crossing by the timber there, and then they are sure to see us."

" Stop," said I, " and now I see what to do. I must get into the water and you must go to sleep."

" To be sure, yes, away in the meadow there. But how bitter cold it will be for you! "

She saw in a moment the way to do it, sooner than I could tell her; and there was no time to lose.

" Now mind you never come again," she whispered over her shoulder as she crept away with a childish twist, hiding her white front from me; " only I shall come sometimes— oh, here they are, Madonna! "

Daring scarce to peep, I crept into the water, and lay down bodily in it, with my head between two blocks of stone, and some flood-drift combing over me. She was lying beneath a rock, thirty or forty yards from me, feigning to be asleep, with her dress spread beautifully, and her hair drawn over her.

Presently one of the great rough men came round a corner upon her; and there he stopped and gazed awhile at her fairness and innocence. Then he caught her up in his arms, and kissed her so that I heard him; and if I had only brought my gun, I would have tried to shoot him.

" Here our queen is! Here's the queen! Here's the captain's daughter!" he shouted to his comrades; " fast asleep, by God, and hearty. Now I have first claim to her; and no one else shall touch the child. Back to the bottle, all of you! "

He set her dainty little form upon his great square shoulder, and her narrow feet in one broad hand; and so in triumph marched away, with the purple velvet of her skirt ruffling in his long black beard, and the silken length of her hair fetched out, like a cloud, by the wind, behind her.

I crept into a bush for warmth, and rubbed my shivering legs on bark, and longed for my mother's fagot. Then as daylight sank below the forget-me-not of stars, with a sorrow to be quit, I knew that now must be my time to get away, if there were any.

Therefore, wringing my sodden breeches, I managed to crawl from the bank to the niche in the cliff, which Lorna had shown me.

Despite the dusk I entered well and held on by some dead fern-stems, but while I was hugging myself, with a boyish manner of reasoning, my joy was as like to have ended in sad grief. For hearing a noise in front of me, and like a coward not knowing where, but afraid to turn round or think of it, I felt myself going down some deep passage, into a pit of darkness. It was no good to catch the sides, for the whole thing seemed to go with me. Then not knowing how, I was leaning over a night of water.

I nearly lost my wits and went to the bottom, but suddenly a robin sang (as they will do after dark towards Spring) in the brown fern and ivy behind me, and gathering quick warm comfort I sprang up the steep way towards the starlight. Climbing back as the stones slid down, I heard the cold greedy wave go lapping like a blind black dog, into the distance of arches, and hollow depths of darkness.

I can assure you and tell no lie, that I scrambled back to the mouth of that pit, as if the evil one had been after me. Thereafter I began to search with the utmost care and diligence, although my teeth were chattering, and all my bones beginning to ache, with the chilliness and the wetness. Before very long the moon appeared over the edge of the mountain and among the trees at the top of it; and then I espied rough steps, and rocky, made as if with a sledge-hammer, narrow, steep, and far asunder, scooped here and there in the side of the entrance, and then round a bulge of the cliff, like the marks upon a great brown loaf, where a hungry child has picked at it. And higher up, where the light of the moon shone broader upon the precipice, there seemed to be a rude broken track. At that moment I saw a movement of lights at the head of the valley, as if lanthorns were coming after me; and the nimbleness given thereon to my heels was in front of all meditation.

Straightway, I set foot in the lowest stirrup (as I might

almost call it), and clung to the rock with my nails, and worked to make a jump into the second stirrup. And I compassed that too, with the aid of my stick; although to tell you the truth, I was not at that time of life so agile as boys of smaller frame are; for my size was growing beyond my years. But the third step-hole was the hardest of all, and the rock swelled out on me, over my breast, and there seemed to be no attempting, until I spied a good stout rope hanging in a groove of shadow, and just managed to reach the end of it.

How I clomb up, and across the clearing, and found my way home through the Bagworthy forest, is more than I can remember now, for I took all the rest of it then as a dream, by reason of perfect weariness.

When I got home, all the supper was in; and the men sitting at the white table, and mother, and Annie, and Lizzie near by, all eager and offering to begin (except, indeed, my mother, who was looking out of the doorway), and by the fire was Betty Muxworthy, scolding and cooking, and tasting her work, all in a breath, as a man would say.

But nobody could get out of me where I had spent all the day and evening; although they worried me never so much, and longed to shake me to pieces; especially Betty Muxworthy, who never could learn to let well alone.

But the fright I had taken that night in Glen Doone made me take care not to wander about the fields without John Fry's company, and I gradually told him all things that had happened to me except, indeed, about Lorna. I was only a boy as yet and inclined to despise young girls and yet my sister Annie was more to me than all the boys of Brendon and Countisbury. And afterwards she grew up to be a very comely maiden, tall, and with a well-built neck, and very fair white shoulders, under a bright cloud of curling hair. But for the present she seemed to me little to look at, after the beauty of Lorna Doone.

4

TOM FAGGUS DESERVES HIS SUPPER

One November evening, when I was about fifteen years old and Annie thirteen we were trying to rescue an old drake who had become trapped and was threatened by flood water, when a man on horseback came suddenly round the corner of the great ash-hedge on the other side of the stream, and his horse's feet were in the water.

" Ho, there," he cried, " get thee back, boy. The flood will carry thee down like a straw. I will do it for thee and no trouble."

With that he leaned forward and spoke to his mare and she entered the flood and he caught up old Tom with his left hand, and set him between his holsters, and smiled at his faint quack of gratitude. In a moment all three were carried down-stream but landed some thirty or forty yards lower, in the midst of our kitchen garden. He would speak to us never a word until he had spoken in full to the mare, as if explaining the whole to her.

" Sweetheart, I know thou couldst have leapt it," he said, as he patted her cheek, being on the ground by this time, and she nudging up to him, with the water pattering off her; " but I had good reason, Winnie dear, for making thee go through it."

She answered him kindly with her soft eyes, and sniffed at him very lovingly, and they understood one another. Then he took from his waistcoat two pepper-corns and made the old drake swallow them. Old Tom stood up quite bravely, and clapped his wings, shook off the wet from his tail feathers and waddled away into the courtyard.

The gentleman turned round to us with a pleasant smile on his face. He was rather short, about John Fry's height or maybe a little taller, but very strongly built and springy, as his gait at every step showed plainly, although his legs were bowed with much riding, and he looked as if he lived on horseback. To a boy like me he seemed very old, being over twenty, and well-found in beard; but he was not more than four and twenty, fresh and ruddy looking, with a short nose, and keen blue eyes, and a merry, waggish jerk about him, as if the world were not in earnest. Yet he had a sharp, stern way, like the crack of a pistol, if anything misliked him; and we knew (for children see such things) that it was safer to tickle than tackle him.

"Well, young uns, what be gaping at?" He gave pretty Annie a chuck in the chin, and took me all in without winking.

"Your mare," said I, standing stoutly up, being a tall boy now: "I never saw such a beauty, sir. Will you let me have a ride of her?"

"Think thou couldst ride her, lad? She will have no burden but mine. Thou couldst never ride her. Tut! I would be loth to kill thee."

"Ride her!" I cried with the bravest scorn, for she looked so kind and gentle; "there never was a horse upon Exmoor foaled, but I could tackle in half an hour. Only I never ride upon saddle. Take them leathers off her."

"I am thy mother's cousin, boy, and am going up to the house. Tom Faggus is my name, as everybody knows; and this is my young mare, Winnie."

What a fool I must have been not to know it at once! Tom Faggus, the great highwayman, and his young blood-mare, the strawberry!

Mr. Faggus gave his mare a wink, and she walked demurely after him.

"Up for it still, boy, be ye?" Tom Faggus stopped, and the mare stopped there; and they looked at me provokingly.

"Is she able to leap, sir? There is a good take-off on this side of the brook."

Mr. Faggus laughed very quietly, turning round to Winnie, so that she might enter into it. And she, for her part, seemed to know exactly where the joke was.

" Not too hard, my dear," he said; " let him gently down on the mixen. That will be quite enough." Then he turned the saddle off and I was up in a moment. But although she tried every device she did not throw me off, though she dragged me through brush and thicket until at last, as she rose at our gate like a bird, I tumbled off into the mixen.

" Well done, lad," Mr. Faggus said good-naturedly; for all were now gathered round me, as I rose from the ground somewhat tottering, and miry and crestfallen, but otherwise none the worse (having fallen upon my head which is of uncommon substance); nevertheless, John Fry was laughing, so that I longed to clout his ears for him. " Not at all bad work, my boy; we may teach you to ride by and by, I see; I thought not to see you stick on so long. . . ."

" I should have stuck on much longer, sir, if her sides had not been wet. She was so slippery. . . ."

" Boy, thou art right. She hath given many the slip! Vex not, Jack, that I laugh at thee. She is like a sweetheart to me, and better than any of them be. It would have gone to my heart if thou hadst conquered. None but I can ride my Winnie mare."

" Foul shame to thee then, Tom Faggus," cried mother, coming up suddenly, and speaking so that all were amazed, having never seen her wrathful; " to put my boy, my boy, across her, as if his life were no more than thine! The only son of his father, an honest man, and a quiet man, not a roystering, drunken robber! "

And she upbraided him and slapped Annie when she remarked on the state of my clothes.

" Winnie shall stop here to-night," said I, for Tom Faggus still said never a word all the while; but began to buckle his things on, for he knew that women are to be met with wool, as the cannon balls were at the siege of Tiverton Castle; " Mother, I tell you Winnie shall stop; else I will go away with her. I never knew what it was, till now, to ride a horse worth riding."

" Young man," said Tom Faggus, still preparing sternly

to depart, " you know more about a horse than any man on Exmoor. Your mother may well be proud of you but she need have no fear. As if I—Tom Faggus, your father's cousin, and the only thing I'm proud of—would ever have let you mount my mare, which dukes and princes have vainly sought, except for the courage in your eyes and the look of your father about you. I knew you could ride when I saw you, and rarely you have conquered. But women care not to understand us. Good bye, John, I am proud of you and I hope to have done you pleasure."

But before he was truly gone out of our yard, my mother came softly after him, with her afternoon apron across her eyes, and her hand ready to offer him. Nevertheless he made as if he had not seen her, though he let his horse go slowly.

" Stop, cousin Tom," my mother said, " a word with you before you go."

" Why bless my heart! " Tom Faggus cried, with the form of his countenance so changed, that I verily thought another man must have leapt into his clothes—" do I see my cousin, Sarah? I thought everyone was ashamed of me, and afraid to offer me shelter since I lost my best cousin, John Ridd." And with that he began to push on again; but my mother would not have it so.

" Ah, Tom, that was a loss indeed. And I am nothing either. And you should try to allow for me; though I never found anyone that did." And mother began to cry, though father had been dead so long; and I looked on with a stupid surprise, having stopped from crying long ago.

" I can tell you one that will," cried Tom, jumping off Winnie in a trice, and looking kindly at mother; " I can allow for you, cousin Sarah, in everything but one. I am in some ways a bad man myself; but I know the value of a good one; and if you gave me orders, by God. . . ." And he shook his fists towards Bagworthy Wood, just heaving up black in the sundown.

" Hush, Tom, hush, for God's sake! " And mother

meant me, without pointing at me; or at least I thought she did. For she ever had weaned me from thoughts of revenge.

"Good night, cousin Sarah; goodnight, cousin Jack," cried Tom, taking to the mare again; "many a mile I have to ride, and not a bit inside of me. No food or shelter this side of Exford, and the night will be black as pitch, I trow. But it serves me right for indulging the lad, being taken with his looks so."

"Cousin Tom," said mother, and trying to get so that Annie and I could not hear her, "it would be a sad and unkin-like thing, for you to despise our dwelling house. We cannot entertain you as the lordly inns on the road do; and we have small change of victuals. But the men will go home, being Saturday; and so you will have the fireside all to yourself and the children."

So Tom Faggus stopped to sup that night with us. He was a jovial soul if ever there has been one. There was about him such a love of genuine human nature, that if a traveller said a good thing, he would give him back his purse again. It is true that he took people's money, more by force than fraud; and the law was bitterly moved against him. These things I do not understand; having seen so much of robbery (some legal, some illegal) that I scarcely know, as here we say, one crow's foot from the other.

"Now let us go and see Winnie, Jack," he said after supper. "For the most part I feed her myself; but she was so hot from the way you drove her. Now she must be grieving for me, and I never let her grieve long."

I was too glad to go with him, and Annie came slyly after us.

"Winnie, Winnie, you little witch," he cried, "we shall die together!"

Then he turned away with a joke and began to feed her nicely, for she was very dainty. Not a husk of oat would she touch, that had been under the breath of another horse, however hungry she might be. And with her oats he mixed some secret powder, and then gave her water and made her bed. So then we said " good-night " to her. Afterwards by the fireside, he kept us very merry, sitting in the great chimney-corner, and making us play games with him.

Cousin Tom set to and told us whole pages of stories, not about his own doings at all; but strangely enough they seemed to concern almost everyone else we had ever heard of. And he changed his face every moment so, and with such power of mimicry, that without so much as a smile of his own, he made even mother laugh so that she broke her new tenpenny waistband; and as for us children, we rolled on the floor, and Betty Muxworthy roared in the wash up.

Mr. Faggus being impoverished in a lawsuit and deprived of his love, had turned to robbery. " The world hath preyed on me, like a wolf. God help me now to prey on the world."

But to us he was kindness itself. He came again about three months afterwards and taught me then how to ride bright Winnie, who was grown since I had seen her, but remembered me most kindly. After making much of Annie, who had a wondrous liking for him, away he went, and young Winnie's sides shone like a cherry by candlelight.

5

MASTER HUCKABACK COMES IN

Now I feel that of those boyish days I have little more to tell, because everything went quietly, as the world for the most part does with us. I began to work at the farm in earnest, and tried to help my mother; and when I remembered Lorna Doone, it seemed no more than the thought of a dream, which I could hardly call to mind. I grew four inches longer in every year of my farming, and a matter of two inches wider; until there was no man of my size to be seen elsewhere upon Exmoor. Little Eliza could never come to a size herself, though she had the wine from the Sacrament, at Easter and All-Hallowmas, only to be small and skinny, sharp and clever crookedly. But Annie, my other sister, was now a fine, fair girl, beautiful to behold.

Now a strange thing came to pass that winter, when I was twenty-one years old, which affrighted the rest, and made me feel uncomfortable. None could explain it, except by attributing it to the devil. The weather was very mild and open, and scarcely any snow fell; at any rate, none lay on the ground even for an hour, in the highest part of Exmoor; a thing which I knew not before or since, as long as I can remember.

At grey of night, when the sun was gone, and no red in the west remained, neither were stars forthcoming, suddenly a wailing voice rose along the valleys, and a sound in the air, as of people running. It mattered not whether you stood on the moor, or crouched behind rocks away from it, or down among reedy places; all as one the sound would come, now from the heart of the earth beneath, now overhead bearing down on you. And then there was rushing of something by, and melancholy laughter, and the hair of a man would stand on end, before he could reason properly. This strange sound made us bar the doors at sunset.

Mr. Reuben Huckaback, whom many good folk in Dulverton will remember long after my time, was my mother's uncle. He owned the very best shop in the town, and did a fine trade in soft-ware, especially when the pack-horses came safely in at Christmas-time. And we being now his only kindred (except indeed, his grand-daughter little Ruth Huckaback, of whom no one took any heed), mother beheld it a Christian duty to keep as well as could be with him, both for love of a nice old man, and for the sake of her children. And truly, the Dulverton people said that he was the richest man in their town, and could buy up half the county armigers.

It had been settled between us, that this old gentleman should spend New-Year with us and we expected him soon after noon on the last day of December. For the Doones being lazy and fond of bed, it was easier to escape them by morning travel but that night they had not gone to bed but rode forth on the Old-Year morning purely in search of mischief.

We had put off our dinner till one o'clock (which to me was a sad foregoing), and there was to be a brave supper at six of the clock, upon New Year's Eve. Our neighbour Nicholas Snowe was to come in the evening, with his three tall, comely daughters, strapping girls and well skilled in the dairy, partly because Mr. Huckaback liked to see fine young maidens, and partly because Nicholas Snowe could smoke a pipe yet all around our parts. And Uncle Ben was a great hand at his pipe, and would sit for hours over it, in our warm chimney-corner, and never want to say a word, unless it were inside him; only he liked to have somebody there over against him smoking.

Now when I came in before one o'clock I fully expected to find Uncle Ben sitting in the fire-place. But there instead of my finding him with his quaint dry face who should run out but Betty Muxworthy, and poke me with a saucepan lid.

" Get out of that now, Betty," I said in my politest manner; for really Betty was now become a great domestic evil. She would have her own way so, and of all the things most distressful was for a man to try to reason with her. I asked her then if Uncle Ben had arrived.

" Raived! I knaws nout about that, whuther a hath or noo. Only I tell'ee, her baint coom. Rackon them Doones hath gat 'un."

And Betty, who hated Uncle Ben, because he never gave her a groat, and she was not allowed to dine with him, I am sorry to say that Betty Muxworthy grinned all across, and poked me again with the greasy sauce-pan cover. But I, misliking so to be treated, strode through the kitchen indignantly and met mother who was very distressed.

" Oh, Johnny, Johnny," she cried, " I am so glad you are come at last. There is something sadly amiss, Johnny."

" Well, mother, what is the matter then ? "

" I am sure you need not be angry, Johnny. You are very

sweet-tempered, I know, John Ridd, but what would you say if the people there "—she would never call them " Doones "—" had gotten your poor Uncle Reuben, horse, and Sunday coat and all ? "

" Why, mother, I should be sorry for them. He would set up a shop by the river-side, and come away with all their money."

" That all you have to say, John! And my dinner done to a very turn, and the supper all fit to go down, and no worry, only to eat and be done with it ! "

" Well, mother dear, I am very sorry. But let us have our dinner. You know we promised not to wait for him after one o'clock. After that I will go to seek for him in the thick of the fog, like a needle in a hay-band."

So we made a very good dinner indeed, though wishing that he could have some of it, and wondering how much to leave for him, and then, as no sound of his horse had been heard, I set out with my gun to look for him with the fog hanging close around me.

After a long ride through the rolling mist I heard a rough low sound, very close in the fog, as of a hobbled sheep a-coughing. I listened and feared, and yet listened again, though I wanted not to hear it.

" Lord have mercy upon me! Oh Lord, upon my soul have mercy! An' if I cheated Sam Hicks last week, Lord knowest how well he deserved it, and lied in every stocking's mouth—oh Lord, where be I a-going ? "

These words with many jogs between them, came to me through the darkness, and then a long groan and a choking. I made towards the sound and presently was met, point-blank, by the head of a mountain pony. Upon its back lay a man, bound down, with his feet on the neck and his head to the tail, and his arms falling down like stirrups.

Before the little horse could turn, I caught him, jaded as he was, by his wet and grizzled forelock. ·

" Good and worthy sir," I said to the man who was riding so roughly: " fear nothing: no harm shall come to thee,"

"Help, good friend, whoever thou art," he gasped, but could not look at me, because his neck was jerked so; "God has sent thee; and not to rob me, because it is done already."

"What, Uncle Ben!" I cried, letting go the horse. "Uncle Ben, here in this plight! What, Mr. Reuben Huckaback!"

"An honest hosier and draper, serge and long-cloth warehouseman"—he groaned from rib to rib—"at the sign of the Gartered Kitten in the loyal town of Dulverton."

"What, Uncle Ben, dost thou not know me, thy dutiful nephew, John Ridd?"

Not to make a long story of it, I cut the thongs that bound him, and set him astride on the little horse; but he was too weak to stay so. Therefore I mounted him on my back, and leading the pony by the cords, which I fastened around his nose, set out for Plover's Barrows.

Now as soon as ever I brought him in, we set him up in the chimney-corner, comfortable and handsome; and it was no little delight to me to get him off my back, for like his own fortune, Uncle Ben was of a good round figure. He gave his long coat a shake or two, and he stamped about in the kitchen, until he was sure of his whereabouts, and then he fell asleep again until supper should be ready.

"He shall marry Ruth," he said by-and-by, to himself and not to me; "he shall marry Ruth for this, and have my little savings, soon as they be worth having. Very little as yet, very little indeed, and ever so much gone today, along of them rascal robbers."

Of course the Doones, and nobody else, had robbed good Uncle Reuben; and then they grew sportive and took his horse, an especially sober nag, and bound the master upon the wild one, for a little change as they told him.

On the following day, Master Huckaback, with some show of mystery, demanded from my mother an escort into a dangerous part of the world, to which his business compelled him. He would not hear of taking our John Fry but

41

insisted that I should go with him. Hereupon my mother grew very pale, and found fifty reasons against my going. Therefore I soon persuaded my mother to let me go, and trust in God; and after that I was greatly vexed to find that this dangerous enterprise was nothing more than a visit to the Baron de Whichehalse to lay an information, and sue a warrant against the Doones, and a posse to execute it.

I could well have told Uncle Reuben that he never would get from Hugh de Whichehalse a warrant against the Doones; moreover, if he did get one, his own wig would be singed with it. But for divers reasons I held my peace, partly from youth and modesty, partly from a desire to see whatever please God I should see.

When we arrived at Ley Manor, the home of Baron de Whichehalse, we were shown very civilly into the hall, and refreshed with good ale, and collared head and the back of a Christmas pudding.

After that, we were called to the Justice-room, where the Baron himself was sitting with Colonel Harding, another Justiciary of the King's Peace, to help him. I had seen the Baron de Whichehalse before, and was not at all afraid of him, having been at school with his son as he knew, and it made him very kind to me.

Hugh de Whichehalse, a white-haired man of very noble presence with friendly blue eyes and a sweet smooth fore-head, and aquiline nose quite beautiful, and thin lips curving delicately, rose as we entered the room; while Colonel Harding turned on his chair, and struck one spur against the other.

Uncle Reuben made his very best scrape, and then walked up to the table, trying to look as if he did not know himself to be wealthier than both the gentlemen put together. Certainly, he was no stranger to them any more than I was; and as it proved afterwards Colonel Harding owed him a lump of money, upon very good security. Of him Uncle Reuben took no notice, but addressed himself to De Whichehalse.

The Baron smiled very gently, as soon as he learned the cause of this visit; and then he replied quite reasonable:

" A warrant against the Doones, Master Huckaback? Which of the Doones, so please you; and the Christian names, what be they ? "

" My lord, I am not their godfather, and most like they never had any. But we all know old Sir Ensor's name, so that may be no obstacle."

" Sir Ensor Doone and his sons—so be it. How many sons, Master Huckaback, and what is the name of each one ? "

" How can I tell you, my lord, even if I had known them all as well as my own shop-boys ? Nevertheless, there were seven of them; and that should be no obstacle."

" A warrant against Sir Ensor Doone, and seven sons of Sir Ensor Doone, Christian names unknown, and doubted if they have any. So far so good, Master Huckaback. I have it all down in writing. Sir Ensor himself was there, of course, as you have given in evidence. . . ."

" No, no, my lord, I never said that; I never said. . . ."

" If he can prove that he was not there, you may be indicted for perjury. But as for those seven sons of his, of course, you can swear that they were his sons, and not his nephews, or grand-children or even no Doones at all."

" My lord, I can swear that they were Doones. Moreover I can pay for any mistake I make. Therein need be no obstacle."

" Oh yes, he can pay; he can pay well enough," said Colonel Harding shortly.

" I am heartily glad to hear it," said the Baron pleasantly; " for it proves after all that this robbery (if robbery there has been) was not so very ruinous. Now, are you quite convinced, good sir, that these people (if there were any) stole or took, or even borrowed anything at all from you ? "

" My lord, do you think that I was drunk ? "

" Not for a moment, Master Huckaback. Although excuse might be made for you, at this time of the year. But how did you know that your visitors were of this particular family?"

"Because it could be nobody else. Because, in spite of the fog. . . ."

"Fog!" cried Colonel Harding sharply.

"Fog!" said the Baron with emphasis. "Ah, that explains the whole affair. I thoroughly understand it now."

"Go back, my good fellow," said Colonel Harding, "and if the day is clear enough, you will find all your things where you left them. I know, from my own experience, what it is to be caught in an Exmoor fog."

Uncle Reuben, by this time, was so put out that he hardly knew what he was saying.

"My lord, Sir Colonel, is this your justice? If I go to London myself for it, the King shall know how his commission—how a man may be robbed, and the justice proved that he ought to be hanged at the back of it; that in this good county of Somerset. . . ."

"Your pardon a moment, good sir," De Whichehalse interrupted him, "but I was about to mention what need be an obstacle. The mal-feasance, if any, was laid in Somerset; but we two humble servants of His Majesty, are in commission of his peace for the County of Devon only, and therefore could never deal with it."

"And why, in the name of God," cried Uncle Reuben, now carried at last fairly out of himself, "why could you not say as much at first, and save me all this waste of time and worry of my temper? Gentlemen, you are all in league; all of you stick together."

Here poor Uncle Ben, not being so strong as before the Doones had played with him, began to foam at the mouth a little, and his tongue went into the hollow, where his short grey whiskers were.

All throughout the homeward road, Uncle Ben had been very silent, feeling much displeased with himself. But before he went to bed that night, he just said to me, "Nephew Jack, you have not behaved so badly as the rest to me. And because you have no gift of talking, I think that I may trust you. Now mark my words, this villain job shall not have ending here. I have another card to play. I will go to the King himself, or a man who is bigger than the King, and to whom I have ready access. I will not tell thee his name at present; only if thou art brought before him, never wilt thou forget it." That was true enough, by-the-by, as I discovered afterwards; for the man he meant was Judge Jeffreys.

" And when are you likely to see him, sir ? "

" Maybe in the Spring, may be not until Summer; for I cannot go to London on purpose, but when my business takes me there. Only remember my words, Jack, and when you see the man I mean, look straight at him and tell no lie. He will make some of your zany squires shake in their shoes, I reckon. Now, I have been in this lonely hole far longer than I intended, by reason of this rage, yet I will stay here one day more, upon a certain condition, that you shall guide me tomorrow, without a word to anyone, to a place where I may well descry the dwellings of these scoundrels Doones, and learn the best way to get at them, when the time shall come. Can you do this for me ? I will pay you well, boy."

I promised very readily to do my best to serve him; but vowed I would take no money for it, not being so poor as that came to.

Accordingly, with Uncle Reuben mounted on my ancient pony, Peggy, I made foot for the westward directly after breakfast. Uncle Ben refused to go unless I would take a loaded gun; and indeed, it was always wise to do so in those days of turbulence.

There was very little said between us, along the lane and across the hill, although the day was pleasant.

I thought of Lorna Doone, the little maid of so many years back, and how my fancy went with her. Could Lorna ever think of me ? Was I not a lout gone by, only fit for loach-sticking ?

We left Peggy when we reached the hill and after much scrambling we at last breasted the hill which formed the side rampart of Glen Doone.

The chine of highland, whereon we stood, curved to the right and left of us, keeping about the same elevation, and crowned with trees and brushwood. At about half a mile in front of us, but looking as if we could throw a stone to strike any man upon it, another crest, just like our own, bowed around to meet it; but failed by reason of two narrow clefts, of which we could only see the brink. One of these clefts was the Doone gate, with a portcullis of rock above it; and the other was the chasm, by which I had made an entrance. Betwixt them, where the hills fell back, as in a perfect oval, traversed by the winding water, lay a bright green valley, rimmed with sheer black rock, and seeming to have sunken bodily from the bleak, rough heights above. It looked as if no frost could enter, neither winds go ruffling; only spring and hope and comfort, breathe to one another.

" See what a pack of fools they be? This great Doone valley may be taken in half-an-hour."

" Yes, to be sure, Uncle; if they like to give it up, I mean."

" Three culverins on yonder hill, and three on the top of this one—and we have them under a pestle. Ah, I have seen the wars, my lad, from Keinton up to Naseby; and I might have been a general now if they had taken my advice."

But I was not attending to him, being drawn away on a sudden by a sight which never struck the sharp eyes of our General. For I had long ago descried that little opening in the cliff, through which I made my exit, as before related, on the other side of the valley. Now, gazing at it with full thought of all that it had cost me, I saw a little figure come, and pause, and pass into it; something very light and white, nimble, smooth and elegant, gone almost before I knew that anyone had been there. And yet my heart came to my ribs, and all my blood was in my face, and pride within me fought with shame, and vanity with self-contempt; for though seven years were gone, and I from boyhood come to manhood, and she must have forgotten me, and I had half-forgotten; at that moment, once for all, I felt that I was face to face with fate (however poor it might be), weal or woe, in Lorna Doone.

6

LORNA BEWITCHES ME

Master Huckaback noticed my confusion and eager gaze at something unseen by him in the valley, and cross-examined me; but I told him nothing of Lorna. He left Plover's Barrows for Dulverton next day, leaving me eagerly planning to visit the Doone Valley again, which indeed I had promised him I would do. I only awaited the slow arrival of some new clothes before setting out, on St. Valentine's Day. I was surprised on this occasion how shallow the Bagworthy Water was and the water slide too; but even so it was after some labour I reached the top and was looking about me when a sweeter note than the thrush or ouzel ever wooed a mate in, floated on the valley breeze. The words were of an ancient song, fit to cry or laugh at.

> " Love, an if there be one,
>   Come, my love to be,
> My love is for the one
>   Loving unto me.
>
> Not for me the show, love,
>   Of a gilded bliss,
> Only thou must know, love,
>   What my value is.
>
> If in all the earth, love,
>   Thou hast none but me,
> This shall be my worth, love,
>   To be cheap to thee.

But, if so thou ever
   Strivest to be free,
'Twill be my endeavour
   To be dear to thee.

Hence may I ensue, love,
   All a woman's due,
Comforting my true love,
   With a love as true."

All this I took in with great eagerness, and presently I ventured to look forth and beheld the loveliest sight.

By the side of the stream she was coming to me, even among the primroses as if she loved them all. I could not see what her face was, only that her hair was flowing from a wreath of white violets. Scarcely knowing what I did, as if a rope were drawing me, I came from the dark mouth of the chasm, and stood, afraid to look at her.

She was turning to fly, not knowing me, and frightened, perhaps, at my stature; when I fell on the grass (as I fell before her seven years agone that day) and I just said: "Lorna Doone!"

She knew me at once from my manner and ways, and a smile broke through her trembling, as sunshine comes through willow leaves; and being so clever, she saw of course, that she needed not to fear me.

"Oh, indeed!" she cried, with a feint of anger (because she had shown her cowardice, and yet in her heart she was laughing); "oh, if you please, who are you, sir, and how do you know my name?"

"I am John Ridd," I answered, "the boy who gave you those beautiful fish, when you were only a little thing, seven years ago today."

"Yes, the poor boy who was frightened so, and obliged to hide in the water."

"And do you remember how kind you were, and saved

my life by your quickness, and went away riding upon a great man's shoulder, as if you had never seen me."

" Oh, yes, I remember everything; because it was so rare to see any, except—I mean, because I happen to remember. But you seem not to remember, sir, how perilous this place is."

For she had kept her eyes upon me; large eyes, of a softness, a brightness, and a dignity, which made me feel as if I must for ever love, and yet forever know myself unworthy. And so I could not answer her, but only waited for the melody of her voice. But she had not the least idea of what was going on in me, any more than I myself had.

" I think, Master Ridd, that you cannot know," she said with her eyes taken from me, " what the dangers of this place are, and the nature of the people."

" Yes, I know enough of that; and I am frightened greatly, all the time when I do not look at you."

So, as she was too young to give coquettish answer, it struck me that I had better go, and have no more to say to her until next time of coming. So would she look the more for me, and think the more about me, and not grow weary of my words, and the want of change there is in me.

" Mistress Lorna, I will depart "—mark you, I thought that a powerful word—" in fear of causing disquiet. If any rogue shot me it would grieve you; I make bold to say it; and it would be the death of my mother. Few mothers have such a son as me. Try to think of me now and then; and I will bring you some new-laid eggs, for our young blue hen is beginning."

" I thank you heartily," said Lorna, " but you need not come to see me. You can put them in my little bower— where I am almost always—I mean whither daily I repair; to think, and to be away from them."

" Only show me where it is. Thrice a day I will come and stop. . . ."

" Nay, Master Ridd, I would never show thee—never, because of peril—only that so happens it, thou hast found the way already."

And she smiled, with a light that made me care to cry out for no other way, only the way to her dear heart. So I touched her white hand softly when she gave it to me; and (fancying that she had sighed) was touched at heart about it, and resolved to yield her all my goods, although my mother was living, and then grew angry with myself (for a mile or more of walking) to think she would condescend so, and then, for the rest of the homeward road, was mad with every man in the world, who would dare to think of looking at her.

That week I could do little more than dream and dream, and rove about, seeking by perpetual change to find the way back to myself.

One thing (more than all the rest) worried and perplexed me. This was that I could not settle, turn and twist it as I might, how soon I ought to go again upon a visit to Glen Doone. For I liked not at all the falseness of it (albeit against murderers), the creeping out of sight and hiding, and feeling as a spy might. And even more than this, I feared how Lorna might regard it; whether I might seem to her a prone and blunt intruder, a country youth not skilled in manners, as among the quality, even when they rob us.

However, when a cold spell in March had passed and spring had come at last, I could restrain myself no more and set out for Glen Doone, regretting that I had not dared tell my sister Annie my secret.

Although my heart was leaping high, with the prospect of some adventure, and the fear of meeting Lorna, I could not but be gladdened by the softness of the weather, and the welcome way of everything.

Going by the waterway, as before, I reached the head ere dark, but fatigued, I lay down and fell alseep. Suddenly my sleep was broken by a shade cast over me; between me and the low sunlight, Lorna Doone was standing.

" Master Ridd, are you mad? " she said, and took my hand to move me.

"Not mad, but half asleep," I answered, feigning not to notice her, that so she might keep hold of me.

"Come away, come away, if you care for your life. The patrol will be here directly. Be quick, Master Ridd, let me hide thee."

"I will not stir a step," said I, though being in the greatest fright that might be well imagined, "unless you call me 'John'."

"Well, John, then—Master John Ridd; be quick if you have any to care for you."

"I have many that care for me," I said, just to let her know; "and I will follow you, Mistress Lorna; albeit without any hurry, unless there be peril to more than me."

Without another word she led me, though with many timid glances, towards the upper valley, into her little bower, where the inlet through the rock was. Inside the niche of native stone, the plainest thing of all to see, at any rate by daylight, was the stairway hewn from rock, and leading up the mountain, by means of which I had escaped, as before related. To the right side of this was the mouth of the pit, still looking very formidable; though Lorna laughed at my fear of it, for she drew her water thence. But on the left was a narrow crevice, very difficult to espy, and having a sweep of grey ivy laid, like a slouching beaver over it. A man here coming from the brightness of the outer air, with eyes dazed by the twilight, would never think of seeing it and following it to its meaning. Lorna raised the screen for me, but I had much ado to pass on account of bulk and stature.

The chamber was unhewn rock, round, as near as might be, eighteen or twenty feet across, and gay with its rich variety of fern, and moss and lichen. Overhead there was no ceiling but the sky itself. The floor was made of soft low grass, mixed with moss and primroses; and in a niche of shelter moved the delicate woodsorrel. Here and there around the sides, were "chairs of living stone" as some Latin writer says; and in the midst a tiny spring arose.

While I was gazing at all these things, with wonder and some sadness, Lorna turned upon me lightly (as her manner was) and said:

" Where are the new-laid eggs, Master Ridd? Or hath thy blue hen ceased laying? "

I did not altogether like the way in which she said it, with a sort of dialect, as if my speech could be laughed at.

" Here be some," I answered, speaking as if in spite of her, " I would have brought thee twice as many, but that I feared to crush them in the narrow ways, Mistress Lorna."

And so I laid her out two dozen upon the moss of the rock ledge, Lorna looking with growing wonder, as I added one to one; and then to my amazement she burst into a flood of tears!

" What have I done? Oh, what have I done to vex you so? "

" It is nothing done by you, Master Ridd," she answered very proudly, as if nought I did could matter; " it is only something that comes upon me, with the scent of the pure, true clover-hay. Moreover, you have been too kind; and I am not used to kindness."

Lorna went a little way; and all my heart gave a sudden jump, to go like a mad thing after her; until she turned of her own accord, and with a little sigh came back to me. Her eyes were soft with trouble's shadow, and the proud lift of her neck was gone.

" Master Ridd," she said in the softest voice that ever flowed between two lips, " have I done aught to offend you? "

Hereupon it went hard with me not to catch her up and kiss her, but Lorna liked me all the better for my good forbearance; because she did not love me yet, and had not thought about it; at least so far as I knew.

But now, because I had behaved so well, Lorna told me all about everything I wished to know, everything she knew, except indeed that point of points, how Master Ridd stood with her.

7

LORNA TELLS HER STORY

" There are but two in the world, who ever listen and try to help me; one of them is my grandfather and the other is the Counsellor. And among the women there are none with whom I can hold converse since my Aunt Sabina died, who took such pains to teach me. She was a lady of high repute and lofty ways and learning, but grieved and harassed more and more by the coarseness and the violence and the ignorance around her.

" For I have no remembrance now of father, or of mother; although they say that my father was the eldest son of Sir Ensor Doone, and the bravest and the best of them. And so they call me heiress to this little realm of violence; and in sorry sport sometimes, I am their Princess or their Queen.

" What I want to know is—what am I, and why set here? I see that you are surprised a little at this my curiosity. Perhaps such questions never spring in any wholesome spirit. But they are in the depths of mine and I cannot be quit of them.

" Meantime, all around me is violence and robbery, coarse delight and savage pain, reckless joke and hopeless death. Is it any wonder that I cannot sink with these, that I cannot so forget my soul, as to live the life of brutes, and die the death more horrible, because it dreams of waking? There is none to lead me forward there is none to teach me right; young as I am, I live beneath a curse that lasts forever."

Here Lorna broke down for a while.

" Master Ridd," she began again, " I am both ashamed and vexed at my own childish folly. It does not happen many times that I give way like this; more shame now to do so, when I ought to entertain you.

" But when I try to search the past, to get a sense of what befell me, ere my own perception formed; to feel back for the lines of childhood, nothing ever comes of it. Nothing, I mean, which I can grasp, and have with any surety; nothing but faint images and wonderment and wandering.

" Often too I wonder at the odds of fortune, which made me (helpless as I am and fond of peace and reading) the heiress of this mad domain, this sanctuary of unholiness. It is not likely that I shall have much power of authority; and yet the Counseller creeps up, to be my Lord of the Treasury; and his son aspires to my hand, as of a Royal alliance.

" We should not be so quiet here, and safe from interruption, but that I have begged one privilege, rather than commanded it. This was, that the lower end, just this narrowing of the valley, where it is most hard to come at, might be looked upon as mine, except for purposes of guard. Therefore none, beside the sentries, ever trespass on me here, unless it be my grandfather, the Counsellor or Carver.

" By your face, Master Ridd, I see that you have heard of Carver Doone. For strength and courage and resource, he bears the first repute among us, as might well be expected from the son of the Counsellor. Among the riders there is none whose safe return I watch for. Neither of the old men is there, whom I can revere or love (except alone my grandfather, whom I love with trembling); neither of the women any whom I like to deal with, unless it be a little maiden whom I saved from starving.

" A little Cornish girl she is, and shaped in western manner; not so very much less in width than if you take her lengthwise. Her father seems to have been a miner, a Cornishman (as she declares) of more than average excellence, yet he left his daughter to starve upon a peat-rick. She looks upon it as a mystery, the meaning of which will some day be clear, and redound to her father's honour. His name was Simon Carfax, the captain of a gang from one of the Cornish tin-mines. Her mother had been buried just a week or so before; and he was sad about it and had been off his work. But in the end he went off to captain another gang and choose the country round. The last she saw of him was this, that he went down a ladder somewhere on the wilds of Exmoor, leaving her with bread and cheese and his travelling hat to see to. And from that day to this, he never came above ground again; so far as we can hear of.

"But Gwenny, holding to his hat, and having eaten the bread and cheese (when he came no more to help her), dwelt three days near the mouth of the hole; and then it was closed over the while she was sleeping. With weakness, and with want of food, she lost herself distressfully, and went away, for miles or more, and lay upon a peat-rick, to die before the ravens.

"Returning from Aunt Sabina's dying-place that very day, very sorrowful, I found this little stray thing lying, with her arms upon her, and not a sign of life, except the way that she was biting. Black root-stuff was in her mouth, and a piece of dirty sheep's wool, and at her feet an old egg-shell of some bird of the moorland.

"I tried to raise her, but she was too square and heavy for me; and so I put food in her mouth, and left her to do right with it. Gwenny ate with delay, and then was ready to eat the basket, and the ware that had contained them.

"Gwenny took me for an angel—though I am little like one, as you see, Master Ridd; and she followed me, expecting that I would open wings and fly, when we came to any difficulty. I brought her home with me; so far as this can be a home; and she made herself my sole attendant, without so much as asking me. She seems to have no kind of fear, even of our roughest men; and yet she looks with reverence and awe upon the Counsellor."

Lorna paused, but I was eager to hear more, and she went on and told me how she was treated.

"My grandfather, Sir Ensor Doone, had given strictest order, as I discovered afterwards, that in my presence all should be well-mannered, kind and vigilant. Nor was it very difficult to keep most part of the mischief from me; for no Doone ever robs at home, neither do they quarrel much, except at times of gambling. And though Sir Ensor Doone is now so old, and growing feeble, his own way he will have still, and no one dare deny him. Under his protection, I am as safe from all those men (some of whom are not akin to me) as if I slept beneath the roof of the King's Lord Justiciary.

"But now, at the time I speak of, one evening of last summer, a horrible thing befell, which took all play of childhood from me. The fifteenth day of last July was very hot and sultry, long after the time of sundown. It was more almost than dusk. At a sudden turn of the narrow path I was following, where it stooped again to the river, a man leaped out from behind a tree, and stopped me, and seized hold of me. I tried to shriek, but my voice was still; and I could only hear my heart.

"'Now, Cousin Lorna, my good cousin,' he said with ease and calmness; 'your voice is very sweet no doubt, from all that I can see of you. But I pray you keep it still, unless you would give to dusty death your very best cousin, and trusty guardian, Alan Brandir of Loch Awe.'

"'You my guardian!' I said, for the idea was too ludicrous.

"'I have in truth that honour, madam,' he answered with a sweeping bow; 'unless I err in taking you for Mistress Lorna Doone.'

"'You have not mistaken me. My name is Lorna Doone.'

"He looked at me with gravity.

"'Then I am your lawful guardian, Alan Brandir of Loch Awe; called Lord Alan Brandir, son of a worthy peer of Scotland. Now will you confide in me?'

"'I confide in you!' I cried, looking at him with amazement. 'Why, you are not older than I am!'

"'Yes, I am, three years at least. You, my ward, are not sixteen. I, your worshipful guardian, am almost nineteen years of age!'

"'I fear that my presence hath scarce enough of ferocity about it,' he gave a jerk to his sword as he spoke, and clanked it on the brook-stones; 'yet do I assure you, cousin, that I am not without some prowess; and many a master of defence hath this good sword of mine disarmed. Now if the boldest and biggest robber in all this charming valley durst so much as breathe the scent of that flower coronal, I would cleave him from head to foot, ere ever he could fly or cry.'

" 'Hush,' I said; 'talk not so loudly, or thou mayest have to do both thyself; and do them both in vain.'

" 'I pray you, be not vexed with me,' he answered in a softer voice; 'for I have travelled far and sorely, for the sake of seeing you. I know right well among whom I stand, and that their hospitality is more of the knife than the salt-stand. Nevertheless, I am safe enough, for my foot is the fleetest in Scotland; and what are such hills as these to me? Tush! I have seen some border forays, among wilder spirits, and craftier men than these be. Once I mind some years agone, when I was quite a stripling lad. . . .'

" 'Worshipful guardian,' I said, 'there is no time now for history. If thou art in no haste, I am, and cannot stay here idling. Only tell me how I am akin and under wardship to thee, and what purpose brings thee here.'

" 'In order, cousin, all things in order, even with fair ladies. First, I am thy uncle's son. For my father, being a leading lord in the councils of King Charles the Second, appointed me to learn the law; not for my livelihood, thank God, but because he felt the lack of it in affairs of state. Of law I learned, as you may suppose, but little; although I have capacities. But the thing was far too dull for me. All I care for is adventure, and found it in our pedigree! I dug down deep in all the branches of our family and have discovered that we, even we, the lords of Loch Awe, have an outlaw for our cousin; and I would we had more, if they be like you.'

" 'Sir' I answered, being amused by his manner, which was new to me (for the Doones are much in earnest), 'surely you count it no disgrace, to be kin to Sir Ensor Doone, and all his honest family! And will you tell me, once for all, sir, how you are my guardian?'

" 'That I will do. You are my ward, because you were my

father's ward, under the Scottish law; and now my father being so deaf, I have succeeded to that right—at least in my opinion—under which claim I am here, to neglect my trust no longer, but to lead you away from scenes and deeds, which are not the best for young gentlewomen. There, spoke I not like a guardian? After that can you mistrust me?'

" 'But,' said I, 'good cousin Alan (if I may so call you) it is not meet for young gentlewomen, to go away with young gentlemen, though fifty times their guardians. But if you will only come with me, and explain your tale to my grandfather, he will listen to you quietly, and take no advanatge of you.'

" 'I thank you very much, kind Mistress Lorna, to lead the goose into the fox's den! But, setting by all thought of danger, I have other reasons against it. Now, come with your faithful guardian, child. I will pledge my honour against all harm, and to bear you safe to London. By the law of the realm I am now entitled to the custody of your fair person, and all your chattels.'

" 'I cannot go, I will not go with you, Lord Alan Brandir,' I answered, being vexed a little by those words of his. 'You are not grave enough for me, you are not old enough for me. My Aunt Sabina would not have wished it; nor would I leave my grandfather without his full permission. I thank you much for coming, sir; but begone at once by the way you came; and pray how did you come, sir?'

" 'Fair cousin, you will grieve for this; you will mourn when you cannot mend it. I would my mother had been here; soon she would have persuaded you. Down the cliffs I came; and up them I must make my way back again. Now adieu, fair cousin Lorna, I see you are in haste tonight; but I am right proud of my guardianship. Give me just one flower for token'—here he kissed his hand to me—and I threw him a truss of woodbine—'adieu, fair cousin, trust me well, I will soon be here again.'

" 'That thou never shalt, sir,' cried a voice as loud as a culverin; and Carver Doone had Alan Brandir, as a spider hath a fly. I heard a sharp sound as of iron and a fall of heavy wood—no unmanly shriek, no cry for mercy."

Here Lorna Doone could tell no more, being overcome with weeping. I could not press her any more with questions, or for clearness; although I longed very much to know whether she had spoken of it to her grandfather, or the Counsellor. And sooth to say, I was not best pleased to be there; and some of Lorna's fright stayed with me, as I talked it away from her.

After hearing that tale from Lorna, I went home in sorry spirits, having added fear for her, and misery about her, to all my other ailments, for now I feared that some young fellow of higher birth might claim her.

But the worst of all was this, that in my anguish to see Lorna weeping so, I had promised not to cause her any further anxiety, which meant that I was not to show myself in the precincts of Glen Doone for at least another month. Should anything happen to increase her present trouble she was to throw a covering of some sort over a large white stone in the entrance to her retreat, which, though unseen from the valley itself, was conspicuous from the height where I stood with Uncle Reuben.

Needless to say, all this time, nothing kept me from looking once a day, and even twice on Sunday, for any sign of Lorna.

8

A ROYAL INVITATION

One afternoon when work was over, a man came riding up, stopped at our gate and stood up from his saddle, and holloed, as if he were somebody; and all the time he was flourishing a white thing in the air.

" Service of the King! " he saith. " Come hither, ____ great yokel, at risk of fine and imprisonment! ____lover Barrows Farm," said he; " God only knows h__ ____red I be.

Is there anywhere in this cursed county a cursed place called 'Plover Barrows Farm'? "

" Sir," I replied, " this is Plover's Barrows Farm, and you are kindly welcome. But why do you think ill of us? We like not to be cursed so."

" Nay, I think no ill," he said; " But I be so galled in the saddle ten days, and never a comely meal of it. And when they hear 'King's service' cried, they give me the worst of everything."

A coarse-grained, hard-faced man he was, some forty years or so, and of middle height and stature. He was dressed in a dark brown riding suit, none the better for Exmoor mud, but fitting him very differently from the fashion of our tailors. Across the holsters lay his cloak, made of some red skin and shining from the sweating of the horse. As I looked down on his stiff bright headpiece, small quick eyes, and black needly beard, he seemed to despise me (too much as I thought) for a mere ignoramus and country bumpkin.

" Annie, have down the cut ham," I shouted; for my sister was come to the door, " and cut a few rashers of hung deer's meat. There is a gentleman come to sup, Annie. And fetch the hops out of the tap with a skewer, that it may run more sparkling."

" I wish I may go to a place never meant for me," said my new friend, now wiping his mouth with the sleeve of his brown coat, " if ever I fell among such good folk, and no error therein. But stay, almost I forgot my business, in the hurry. Hungry I am, and sore of body, from my heels right upward, and sorest in front of my doublet; yet may I not rest, nor bite barley-bread, until I have seen and touched John Ridd. God grant that he be not far away; I must eat my saddle if it be so."

" Have no fear, good sir," I answered; " you have seen and touched John Ridd. I am he, and not one likely to go beneath a bushel."

" It would take a large bushel to hold thee, John Ridd. In

the name of the King, His Majesty, Charles the Second, these presents!"

He touched me with the white thing which I now beheld to be sheepskin, such as they call parchment. It was tied across with cord, and fastened down in every corner with unsightly dabs of wax. By order of the messenger (for I was over-frightened now to think of doing anything) I broke enough of seals to keep an Easter ghost from rising; and there I saw my name in large; God grant such another shock may never befall me in my old age.

" If you please, sir, what is your name?" I asked; though why I asked him I know not, except from fear of witchcraft.

" Jeremy Stickles is my name, lad, nothing more than a poor apparitor of the worshipful Court of King's Bench. And at this moment a starving one, and no supper for me, unless thou wilt read."

Being compelled in this way, I read the King's command to appear before Judge Jeffreys at Westminster at government expense to give evidence.

The messenger was surprised that I could read so much, but I became giddy with a noise in my ears.

" My son, be not afraid," said the messenger; " we are not going to skin thee. Only thou tell all the truth, and it shall be—but never mind, I will tell thee all about it, and how to come out harmless."

Master Jeremy Stickles (no bad man, after all) explained to my mother, that the King on his throne was unhappy until he had seen John Ridd. That the fame of John had gone so far, and his size, and all his virtues—that verily by the God who made him, the King was overcome with it.

Then mother lay back in her garden chair, and smiled upon the whole of us, and most of all on Jeremy. But I myself was deeply gone into the pit of sorrow. For what would Lorna think of me? Here was the long month just expired, there would be her lovely self, peeping softly down the glen, yet there would be nobody to meet her! Dwelling upon this and seeing no chance of escape from it, I could not find one wink of sleep; though Jeremy Stickles (who slept close by) snored loud enough to spare me some. For I felt myself to be, as it were, in a place of some importance; in a situation of trust I may say, and bound not to depart from it. For who could tell what the King might have to say to me about the Doones—and I felt that they were at the bottom of this strange appearance—or what His Majesty might think, if after receiving a message from him I were to violate his faith in me as a churchwarden's son, and falsely spread his words about.

But although Master Stickles was in no hurry to leave that day I could not persuade him to stay beyond Friday. He insisted that we start off on the Saturday morning. Therefore my only chance of seeing Lorna, before I went, lay in watching from the cliff and espying her, or a signal from her. This, however, I did in vain, until my eyes were weary.

It would have taken ten King's Messengers to get me away from Plover's Barrows, without one goodbye to Lorna, but for my sense of the trust which His Majesty had reposed in me.

Jeremy, seeing how much I was down, did his best to keep me up with jokes, and tales, and light discourse, until, before we had ridden a league, I began to long to see the things he was describing.

It was a long and weary journey. In consequence of the pass we had, and the vintners' knowledge of it, we only met two public riders, one of whom made off straightway when he saw my companion's pistols and the stout carbine I bore; and the other came to a parley with us; and proved most kind and affable, when he knew himself in the presence of the cousin of Tom Faggus.

The night was falling very thick by the time we were come to Tyburn, and here the King's officer decided that it would be wise to halt; because the way was unsafe by night across the fields to Charing village. I for my part was nothing loth, and preferred to see London by daylight.

And after all, it was not worth seeing, but a very hideous

and dirty place, not at all like Exmoor. The only things that pleased me much were the River Thames, and the hall and church of Westminster, where there are brave things to be seen, and braver still to think about. But whenever I wandered in the streets, what with the noise the people made, the number of the coaches, the running of the footmen, the swaggering of great courtiers, and thrusting aside of everybody, many and many a time I longed to be back among the sheep again, for fear of losing temper.

Now this being the year of Our Lord 1683, more than nine years and a half since the death of my father, and the beginning of this history, all London was in a great ferment, about the dispute between the Court of the King and the City. This kept me hanging on much longer because the officers of the King's Bench, to whom I daily applied myself, were in counsel with their fellows, and put me off from day to day.

At length, being quite at the end of my money, and seeing no other help for it, I determined to listen to clerks no more, but force my way up to the Justices in Westminster, and insist upon being heard by them, or discharged from my recognizance; for so they had termed the bond or deed which I had been forced to execute, in the presence of a chief clerk or notary, the very day after I came to London. And the support of this bond was, that on pain of a heavy fine, I would hold myself ready and present, to give evidence when called upon. Having delivered me up to sign this, Jeremy Stickles was quit of me, and went upon other business; not but what he was kind and good to me, when his time and pursuits allowed of it.

9

A GREAT MAN ATTENDS TO BUSINESS

In Westminster Hall I found nobody. And at last an old man told me that all the lawyers were gone to see the result of their own works, in the fields of Lincoln's Inn. However, in a few days' time I had better fortune and was taken to the head clerk. When this gentleman understood all about my business (which I told him without complaint) he frowned at me very heavily, as if I had done him an injury.

" John Ridd," he asked me with a stern glance, " is it your deliberate desire to be brought into the presence of the Lord Chief Justice ? "

" Surely, sir, it has been my desire for the last two months and more."

" Then, John, thou shalt be. Now, if my Lord cross-question you, answer him straight out truth at once, for he will have it out of thee. And mind, he loves not to be contradicted, neither can he bear a hang-dog look. Take little heed of the other two, but note every word of the middle one; and never make him speak twice."

I thanked him for his good advice, as he moved the curtain and thrust me in, but instead of entering withdrew, and left me to bear the brunt of it.

The chamber was not very large, though lofty to my eyes, and dark, with wooden panels round it and at the farther end were some raised seats. There were only three men sitting there, one in the centre and one at each side; and all three were done up wonderfully with fur, and robes of state, and curls of thick grey horse-hair, crimped and gathered, and down to their shoulders. Each man had an oak desk before him, set at a little distance, and spread with pens and papers. Instead of writing, however, they seemed to be laughing and talking, or rather the one in the middle seemed to be telling some good story, which the others received with approval. By reason of their great perukes, it was hard to tell how old they were; but the one who was speaking seemed the youngest, although he was the chief of them. A thick-set, burly and bulky man, with a blotched broad face, and great square jaws, and fierce eyes full of blazes; he was one to be dreaded by gentle souls, and to be abhorred by the noble.

Between me and the three Lord Judges, some few lawyers were gathering up bags and papers and pens and so forth, from a narrow table in the middle of the room; as if a case had been disposed of and no other were called on. But before I had time to look round twice, the stout, fierce man espied me, and shouted out with a flashing stare:

" How now, countryman, who art thou ? "

" May it please your worship," I answered him loudly, " I am John Ridd of Oare parish, in the county of Somerset, brought to this London, some two months back by a special messenger, whose name is Jeremy Stickles; and then bound over to be at hand and ready, when called upon to give evidence, in a matter unknown to me, but touching the peace of our lord the King and the well-being of his subjects. Three times I have met our Lord the King, but he hath said nothing about his peace, and only held it towards me; and every day, save Sunday, I have walked up and down the great hall of Westminster, all the business part of the day, expecting to be called upon. And now I desire to ask your worship, whether I may go home again ? "

" Well done, John," replied his lordship, while I was panting with all this speech; " I will go bail for thee, John, thou hast never made such a long speech before; and thou art a brave Briton, or thou couldst not have made it now. I remember the matter well; and I myself will attend to it, although it arose before my time "—he was but newly Chief Justice—" but I cannot take it now, John. Be thou here again tomorrow; and before any other case is taken, I will see justice done to thee. Now be off, boy; thy name is Ridd and we are well rid of thee."

I was only too glad to go after all this tempest; as you may well suppose. For if ever I saw a man's eyes become two holes for the devil to glare through, I saw it that day; and the eyes were those of the Lord Chief Justice Jeffreys.

Next morning I arrived at Westminster Hall feeling apprehensive, but was relieved to see the clerk smiling. He came up to me and whispered confidentially:

" He is all alone this morning, John, and in rare good humour. He hath been promised the handling of poor

Master Algernon Sidney, and says he will soon make republic of him; for his state shall shortly be headless. He is chuckling over his joke, like a pig with a nut; and that always makes him pleasant. John Ridd, my lord;" and with that he swung up the curtain bravely, and according to special orders, I stood face to face, and alone with Judge Jeffreys.

His lordship was busy with some letters, and did not look up for a minute or two, although he knew that I was there. Meanwhile I stood waiting to make my bow; afraid to begin upon him, and wondering at his great bull head. Then he closed his letters, well pleased with their import, and fixed his bold, broad stare on me, as if I were an oyster opened, and he would know how fresh I was.

" May it please your worship," I said, " here I am according to order, awaiting your good pleasure."

" Thou art made to weight, John, more than order. How much dost thou tip the scales to ? "

" Only twelve score pounds, my lord, when I be in wrestling trim. And sure I must have lost weight here, fretting so long in London."

" Now John, or Jack, as thou art more used to be called, we will proceed to examine thee." Here all his manner was changed, and he looked with heavy brows bent upon me, as if he had never laughed in his life, and would allow none else to do so.

" I am ready to answer, my lord," I replied, " if he asks me naught beyond my knowledge, or beyond my honour."

" Hadst better answer me everything, lump. What hast thou to do with honour ? Now is there in thy neighbourhood a certain nest of robbers, miscreants and outlaws, whom all men fear to handle ? "

" Yes, my lord."

" What is the name of this pestilent race, and how many are there ? "

" They are the Doones of Bagworthy forest, may it please

your worship. And we reckon there be about forty of them, beside the women and children."

"Forty Doones! All forty thieves; and women and children! Thunder of God! How long have they been there then?"

"They may have been there thirty years, my lord; and indeed they may have been forty. Before the great war broke out they came, longer back than I can remember."

"Ay, long before thou wast born, John. Good, thou speakest plainly. There is also a family called De Whichehalse living very nigh thee, John?"

This he said in a sudden manner, as if to take me off my guard.

"Yes, my lord, there is. At least, not so very far from us. Baron de Whichehalse, of Ley Manor."

"Baron, ha, of the Exchequer, eh, lad? And taketh dues instead of His Majesty. Riotous knaves in West England, drunken outlaws, you shall dance, if ever I play pipe for you."

"Although your worship is so learned," I answered, seeing that now he was beginning to make things uneasy, "your worship, though being Chief Justice does little justice to us. We are downright, good and loyal folk; and I have not seen since here I came to this great town of London, any who may better us, or even come anigh us in honesty, and goodness, and duty to our neighbours. For we are very quiet folk, not prating our own virtues. . . ."

"Enough, good John, enough! Now hast thou ever heard or thought, that De Whichehalse is in league with the Doones of Bagworthy?"

The idea was so new to me, that it set my wits all wandering; and looking into me, he saw that I was groping for the truth.

"John Ridd, thine eyes are enough for me. I see thou hast never dreamed of it. Now hast thou ever seen a man, whose name is Thomas Faggus?"

"Yes, sir, many and many a time. He is my own worthy

cousin; and I fear that he hath intentions . . ." here I stopped, having no right there to speak about our Annie.

"Tom Faggus is a good man," he said, and his great square face had a smile which showed me he had met my cousin; "Master Faggus hath made mistakes as to the title to property, as lawyers sometimes may do; but take him all for all. he is a thoroughly straightforward man; presents his bill and has it paid, and makes no charge for drawing it. Nevertheless, we must tax his costs as of any other solicitor."

"To be sure, to be sure, my lord!" was all that I could say, not understanding what all this meant.

"I fear he will come to the gallows," said the Lord Chief Justice, sinking his voice below the echoes; "tell him this from me, Jack. He shall never be condemned before me; but I cannot be everywhere; and some of our Justices may keep short memory of his dinners. Tell him to change his name, turn parson, or do something else to make it wrong to hang him. Parson is the best thing; he hath such command of features, and he might take his tithes on horseback. Now a few more things, John Ridd; and for the present I have done with thee."

All my heart leapt up at this, to get away from London so; and yet I could hardly trust to it.

"Is there any sound round your way of disaffection to His Majesty, His most gracious Majesty?"

"No, my lord, no sign whatever. We pray for him in church, perhaps; and we talk about him afterwards, hoping it may do him good as it is intended. But after that we have nought to say, not knowing much about him—at least till I get home again."

"That is as it should be, John. And the less you say the better. But I have heard of things in Taunton, and even nearer to you in Dulverton, and even nigher still upon Exmoor; things which are of the pillory kind, and even more of the gallows. I see that you know nought of them. Nevertheless, it will not be long before all England hears of them. Now, John, I have taken a liking to thee; for never man told me the truth, without fear or favour, more thoroughly and truly than thou hast done. Keep thou clear of this, my son. It will come to nothing; yet many shall swing high for it. Even I could not save thee, John Ridd, if thou wert mixed in this affair. Keep from the Doones, keep from De Whichehalse, keep from everything which leads beyond the sight of thy knowledge. I meant to use thee as my tool; but I see thou art too honest and simple. I will send a sharper down; but never let me find thee, John, either a tool for the other side, or a tube for my words to pass through."

Here the Lord Justice gave me such a glare, that I wished myself well rid of him, though thankful for his warnings; and seeing how he had made upon me a long abiding mark of fear, he smiled again in a jocular manner and said:

" Now get thee gone, Jack. I shall remember thee; and I trow thou wilt not for many a day forget me."

Although I had had money given me by a clerk of the court to cover my costs in London, when I went to ask for the money to take me back to Exmoor the clerk refused to have anything to do with me. But I was saved from having to beg my way home; for going to buy, with my last crown piece, a little shot and powder, more needful on the road almost than even shoes or victuals, at the corner of the street I met my good friend Jeremy Stickles, newly come in search of me. I took him back to my little room—mine at least till tomorrow morning—and told him all my story, and how much I felt aggrieved by it. But he surprised me very much, by showing no surprise at all.

" It is the way of the world, Jack. They have gotten all they can from thee, and why should they feed thee further? Thou art a lucky man, John; though hast gotten one day's wages, or at any rate, half a day, after thy work was rendered. Five pounds thou shalt have, Jack. Ten I would have made it, John, but for bad luck lately. Put back your bits of paper, lad; I will have no acknowledgement. John Ridd, no nonsense with me! "

For I was ready to kiss his hand, to think that any man in

London (the meanest and most suspicious place upon all God's earth) should trust me with five pounds, without even a receipt for it!

It was the beginning of wheat-harvest, when I came to Dunster town; and when I crossed Exmoor, rejoicing to see my own land again, Annie was the first to greet me at Plover's Barrows.

" I knew you would come. Oh, John! Oh, John! I have waited here every Saturday night; and I saw you for the last mile or more."

10

JOHN HAS HOPE OF LORNA

I felt much inclined to tell dear mother all about Lorna, and how I loved her, yet had no hope of winning her; but the thought of father's terrible death at the hands of the Doones prevented me. If once Lorna loved me, my mother should know it; but I saw no more chance of Lorna loving me, than of the man in the moon coming down. So on Monday morning, without a word to anyone, I strode right away towards Doone Glen, in good trust of my speed, without any more misgivings; but resolved to face the worst of it and try to be home for supper.

And first I went, I know not why, to the crest of the broken highland, whence I had agreed to watch for any mark or signal. And sure enough at last I saw (when it was too late to see) that the white stone had been covered over with a cloth or mantle—the sign that something had arisen to make Lorna want me. Then off I set, with small respect for my knees or neck, to make the round of the outer cliffs, and come up my old access.

Nothing could stop me; it was not long, although to me it seemed an age, before I stood in the niche of the rock at the head of the slippery watercourse, and gazed into the quiet glen.

At last a little figure came, not insignificant (I mean), but looking very light and slender in the moving shadows, gently here and softly there, as if vague of purpose, in and out of the wealth of trees, and liberty of the meadow.

I went slowly towards her, taken aback in my impulse; and said all I could come to say, with some distress in doing it.

"Mistress Lorna, I had hope that you were in need of me."

"Oh, yes, but that was long ago; two months or more, sir." And saying this she looked away, as if it were over. And I tried to turn away, without another word, and go.

But I could not help one stupid sob; it came too sharp for pride to stay it, and it told a world of things. Lorna heard it and ran to me, with her bright eyes full of wonder, pity and great kindness, as if amazed that I had more than a simple liking for her. Then she held out both hands to me; and I took and looked at them.

"Master Ridd. I did not mean," she whispered very softly, "I did not mean to vex you."

"If you would be loth to vex me, none else in this world can do it," I answered out of my great love, but fearing yet to look at her, mine eyes not being strong enough.

"Come away from this bright place," she answered, trembling in her turn; "I am watched and spied of late. Come beneath the shadows, John."

She led me to her own rich bower, which I told of once before; I left her quite alone; though close, though tingling to have hold of her. Even her right hand was dropped and lay among the mosses. Neither did I try to steal one glimpse below her eyelids. Life and death were hanging on the first glance I should win; yet I let it be so.

After long or short—I know not, yet ere I was weary, ere I yet began to think or wish for any answer—Lorna raised her eyelids slowly, with a gleam of dew beneath them, and looked at me doubtfully. Any look with so much in it never met my gaze before.

" Darling, do you so love me ? " was all that I could say to her.

" Yes, I like you very much," she answered, with her eyes gone from me, and her dark hair falling over, so as not to show me things.

" But do you love me, Lorna, Lorna; do you love me more than all the world ? "

" No, to be sure not. Now why should I ? "

" In truth, I know not why you should. Only I hoped that you did. Lorna. Either love me not at all, or as I love you, for ever."

" John, I love you very much; and I would not grieve you. You are the bravest, and the kindest, and the simplest of all men—I mean of all people; I like you very much, Master Ridd, and I think of you almost every day."

" That will not do for me, Lorna. Not almost every day I think, but every instant of my life, I think of you. For you I would give up my home, my love of all the world beside, my duty to my dearest ones; for you I would give up my life, and hope of life beyond it. Do you love me so ? "

" Not by any means," said Lorna; " no; I like you very much when you do not talk so wildly; and I like to see you come as if you would fill our valley up, and I like to think that even Carver would be nothing in your hands—but as to liking you like that, what should make it likely ? Especially when I have made the signal, and for some two months or more, you have never even answered it! If you like me so ferociously, why do you leave me for other people to do just as they like with me ? "

" To do as they like! Oh, Lorna, not to make you marry Carver ? "

" No, Master Ridd, be not frightened so; it makes me fear to look at you "

" But you have not married Carver yet ? Say quick! Why keep me waiting so ? "

" Of course I have not, Master Ridd. Should I be here if I had, think you, and allowing you to like me so, and to hold my hand, and make me laugh, as I declare you almost do sometimes? And at other times you frighten me."

" Did they want you to marry Carver? Tell me all the truth of it."

" Not yet, not yet. They are not half so impetuous as you are, John. I am only just seventeen, you know, and who is to think of marrying? But they wanted me to give my word, and be formally betrothed to him in the presence of my grandfather. It seems that something frightened them. There is a youth named Charleworth Doone, everyone calls him 'Charlie'; a headstrong and gay young man, very gallant in his looks and manner; and my uncle, the Counsellor, chose to fancy that Charlie looked at me too much, coming by my grandfather's cottage."

Here Lorna blushed so that I was frightened, and began to hate this Charlie more, a great deal more, than even Carver Doone.

" He had better not," said I; " I will fling him over it, if he dare. He shall see thee through the roof, Lorna, if at all he sees thee."

" Master Ridd, you are worse than Carver! I thought you were so kind-hearted. Well, they wanted me to promise and even to swear a solemn oath (a thing I have never done in my life) that I would wed my eldest cousin, this same Carver Doone, who is twice as old as I am, being thirty-five and upwards. That was why I gave the token that I wished to see you, Master Ridd. They pointed out how much it was for the peace of all the family, and for mine own benefit; but I would not listen for a moment, though the Counsellor was most eloquent, and my grandfather begged me to consider, and Carver smiled his pleasantest, which is a truly frightful thing. Then both he and his crafty father were for using force with me; but Sir Ensor would not hear of it; and they have put off that extreme, until he shall be past its knowledge, or, at least, beyond preventing it. And now I am watched, and spied, and followed, and half my little liberty seems to be taken from me. I could not be here speaking with you even in my own nook and refuge, but for the aid, and skill, and courage of dear little Gwenny Carfax. She is now my chief reliance, and through her alone I hope to baffle all my enemies, since others have forsaken me."

Tears of sorrow and reproach were lurking in her soft dark eyes, until in fewest words I told her, that my seeming negligence was nothing but my bitter loss and wretched absence far away; of which I had so vainly striven to give any tidings without danger to her. When she heard all this, and saw what I had brought from London (which was nothing less than a ring of pearls with a sapphire in the midst of them, as pretty as could well be found) she let the gentle tears fall fast, and came and sat so close beside me, that I trembled like a folded sheep at the bleating of her lamb. But recovering comfort quickly, without more ado, I raised her left hand, and before she could say a word, on her finger was my ring—sapphire for the veins of blue, and pearls to match white fingers.

" Oh, you crafty Master Ridd! " said Lorna, looking up at me, and blushing now a far brighter blush than when she spoke of Charlie; " I thought that you were much too simple ever to do this sort of thing. No wonder you can catch the fish, as when first I saw you."

" Have I caught you, little fish? Or must all my life be spent in hopeless angling for you? "

" Neither one, nor the other, John! You have not caught me yet altogether, though I like you dearly, John; and if you will only keep away, I shall like you more and more. As for hopeless angling, John—that all others shall have until I tell you otherwise."

With the large tears in her eyes—tears which seemed to me to rise partly from her want to love me with the power of my love—she put her pure bright lips, half smiling, half prone to reply to tears, against my forehead lined with trouble, doubt, and eager longing And then she drew my ring from off that snowy twig, her finger, and held it out to me; and then, seeing how my face was falling, thrice she touched it with her lips, and sweetly gave it back to me. "John, I dare not take it now; else I should be cheating you. I will try to love you dearly, even as you deserve and wish. Keep it for me just till then. Something tells me I shall earn it in a very little time. Perhaps you will be sorry then, sorry when it is all too late, to be loved by such as I am."

She would not let me revile myself, telling me my learning was much greater than hers. At last she said:

"Now, John," being so quick that not even a lover could cheat her, and observing my confusion at her use of my Christian name more intently than she need have done. "Master John Ridd, it is high time for you to go home to your mother. I love your mother very much, from what you have told me about her, and I will not have her cheated."

"If you truly love my mother," said I very craftily, "the only way to show it is by truly loving me."

Upon that, she laughed at me in the sweetest manner, and with such provoking ways, and such come-and-go of glances, and beginning of quick blushes, which she tried to laugh away, that I knew, as well as if she herself had told me, that Lorna Doone had now begun, and would go on, to love me.

Although I was under interdict for two months from my darling—"one for your sake, one for mine" she had whispered, with her head withdrawn, yet not so very far from me—lighter heart was not on Exmoor than I bore for half the time, and even for three-quarters. For she was safe; I knew that daily by a mode of signals, well-contrived between us now, on the strength of our experience. "I have nothing now to fear, John," she had said to me, as we parted; "it is true that I am spied and watched, but Gwenny is too keen for them. While I have my grandfather to prevent all violence; and little Gwenny to keep watch on those who try to watch me; and you above all others, John, ready at a moment, if the worst comes to the worst—this neglected Lorna Doone was never in such case before. Therefore do not squeeze my hand, John; I am safe without it, and you do not know your strength."

11

ANNIE GETS THE BEST OF IT

One evening, it was the night of our Harvest revels, I stole away from the crowd that had assembled in our courtyard, to get a change from the noise and the merry-making. Making my way to father's grave I was surprised to see Annie there, but deemed it a good opportunity to find out more of her affairs with Tom Faggus.

" My poor Annie, have you really promised him to be his wife? "

Annie, however, was in a mood to taunt me about Sally Snowe, daughter of our neighbour.

" Then after all you have no reason, John, no particular reason I mean, for slighting poor Sally Snowe so? "

" Without even asking mother or me! Oh, Annie, it was wrong of you! "

" But, darling, you know that mother wishes you so much to marry Sally; and I am sure you could have her tomorrow. She dotes on the very ground. . . ."

" I dare say he tells you that, Annie, that he dotes on the ground you walk on—but did you believe him, child? "

" You may believe me, I assure you, John; and half the farm to be settled upon her, after the old man's time; and though she gives herself little airs, it is only done to entice you; she has the very best hand in the dairy, John, and the lightest at a turnover cake. . . ."

" Now, Annie, don't talk nonsense so. I wish just to know the truth about you and Tom Faggus. Do you mean to marry him? "

" I to marry before my brother, and leave him with none to take care of him! Who can do him a red deer collop, except Sally herself, as I can? Come home, dear, at once, and I will do one for you; for you never ate a morsel of supper, with all the people you had to attend upon."

This was true enough, and seeing no chance of anything more than cross questions and crooked purposes, at which a girl was sure to beat me, I even allowed her to lead me home, with thoughts of the collop uppermost. But the young hussy stopped at the farmyard gate, and jerked out quite suddenly:

" Can your love do a collop, John ? "

" No, I should hope not," I answered rashly; " she is not a mere cook-maid, I should hope."

" She is not half so pretty as Sally Snowe, I will answer for that," said Annie.

" She is ten thousand times as pretty as ten thousand Sally Snowes," I replied with great indignation.

" Oh, but look at Sally's eyes !" cried my sister rapturously.

" Look at Lorna Doone's," said I, " and you would never look again at Sally's."

" Oh, Lorna Doone, Lorna Doone!" exclaimed our Annie, half-frightened, yet clapping her hands with triumph at having found me out so; " Lorna Doone is the lovely maiden, who has stolen poor somebody's heart so. Ah, I shall remember it because it is so queer a name."

" Well," I replied, " it is no use crying over spilt milk, Annie. You have my secret and I have yours; and I scarcely know which of the two of us is likely to have the worst time of it, when it comes to mother's ears. I could put up with perpetual scolding; but not with mother's sad silence."

" That is exactly how I feel, John," and as Annie said it she brightened up, and her soft eyes shone upon me; " but now I shall be much happier, dear; because I shall try to help you."

We entered the house quite gently thus, and found Farmer Nicholas Snowe asleep, little dreaming how his plans had been overset between us. And then Annie said to me very slyly, between a smile and a blush: " Don't you wish Lorna Doone was here, John, in the parlour along with mother, instead of those two fashionable milkmaids, as Uncle Ben will call them, and poor stupid Mistress Kebby ? "

" That indeed I do, Annie."

" She loves you with all her heart, John. No doubt about that, of course."

And so dear Annie, having grown quite brave, gave me a little push into the parlour, where I was quite abashed to enter, after all I had heard about Sally. But they all talked so grandly that I knew there must be somebody in the room besides Jasper Kebby to talk at.

And so there was; for behind the curtain drawn across the window-seat, no less a man than Uncle Ben was sitting half-asleep and weary; and by his side a little girl, very quiet and very watchful. My mother led me to Uncle Ben, who in answer to my greeting said: " Well enough, for that matter; but none the better for the noise you great clods have been making."

" I am sorry if we have disturbed you, sir," I answered very civilly, " but I knew not that you were here even; and you must allow for harvest time."

" So it seems," he replied, " and allow a great deal, including waste and drunkenness. Now (if you can see so small a thing, after emptying flagons much larger) this is my granddaughter, and my heiress "—here he glanced at mother—" my heiress, little Ruth Huckaback."

" I am very glad to see you, Ruth," I answered, offering her my hand, which she seemed afraid to take; " welcome to Plover's Barrows, my good cousin Ruth."

However, my good cousin Ruth only arose, and made me a courtesy, and lifted her great brown eyes at me, more in fear, as I thought than in kinship. And if ever anyone looked unlike the heiress to great property, it was the little girl before me.

" Come out to the kitchen, dear, and let me chuck you to the ceiling," I said just to encourage her; " I always do it to little girls; and then they can see the hams and bacon." But Uncle Reuben burst out laughing; and Ruth turned away with a deep, rich colour.

" Do you know how old she is, you numskull ? " said

Uncle Ben in his driest drawl; " she was seventeen last July, sir."

" On the first of July, grandfather," Ruth whispered, with her back still to me; " but many people will not believe it."

Here mother came up to my rescue, as she always loved to do; and she said: " If my son may not dance Miss Ruth, at any rate he may dance with her. We have only been waiting for you, dear John, to have a little harvest dance, with the kitchen door thrown open. You take Ruth; Uncle Ben take Sally; Master Kebby pair off with Polly; and neighbour Nicholas will be good enough, if I can awake him, to stand up with fair Mistress Kebby. Lizzie will play us the virginal. Won't you, Lizzie, dear ? "

We all started to dance and I was surprised that mother did all she could to prevent me talking to Sally Snowe, the very opposite of what she used to do, and kept me with Ruth Huckaback all the evening.

Then Annie came sailing down the dance, blushing, with her fair cheeks red beneath her dear blue eyes, as she met my glance of surprise at the partner she was leaning on. It was Squire Marwood de Whichehalse, who had come in with Parson Bowden. I whispered that she had no right to be dancing with any other but Tom Faggus. She only said: " See to yourself, John. No, but let us both enjoy ourselves. You are not dancing with Lorna, John. But you seem uncommonly happy."

" Tush," I said; " could I flip about so, if I had my love with me ? "

Being forced to be up before daylight next day, in order to begin right early, I would not go to my bedroom that night for fear of disturbing my mother, but determined to sleep in the loft awhile, the place being cool, and airy, and refreshing with the smell of sweet hay. But as I stood in the court wondering awhile at the glory of the harvest moon, I saw a short wide figure glide across the foot of the courtyard, between me and the six-barred gate. Instead of running after it, as I should have done, I began to consider who it could be, and what on earth it was doing there.

Having made up my mind at last, that it could be none of our people—though not a dog was barking—and also that it must have been either a girl or a woman, I ran down with all speed to learn what might be the meaning of it. But I came too late for this was the lower end of the courtyard, where the brook goes down to the Lynn stream, where Squire Faggus had saved the old drake. And here there was plenty of place to hide.

I saw at once that it was vain to make any pursuit by moonlight; and resolving to hold my own council about it (though puzzled not a little) and to keep watch there another night, back I returned to the loft ladder, and slept without leaving off till morning.

Now many people may wish to know, as indeed I myself did very greatly, what had brought Master Huckaback over from Dulverton, at that time of year when the clothing business was most active on account of harvest wages.

He seemed in no hurry to take his departure, though his visit was so inconvenient to us, as himself indeed must have noticed.

We could not but think, the times being wild and disjointed, that Uncle Ben was not using fairly the part of a guest in our house, to make long expeditions we knew not whither, and to involve us in trouble we knew not what.

For his mode was directly after breakfast to pray to the Lord a little (which used not to be his practice) and then to go forth upon Dolly, Annie's quiet pony, with a bag of good victuals hung behind him, and two great cavalry pistols in front. And he always wore his meanest clothes, as if expecting to be robbed, or to disarm the temptation thereto; and he never took his golden chronometer, neither his bag of money. So much the girls found out and told me. For he never returned until dark or more, just in time to be in before us, who were coming home from the harvest. And then Dolly always seemed very weary, and stained with a muck from beyond our parish. But I refused to follow him.

Thereupon, the girls knowing my way, ceased to torment

me about it; but what was my astonishment, the very next day to perceive that instead of fourteen reapers, we were only thirteen left.

" Who has been and left his scythe ? " I asked; " and here's a tin cup never handled! "

" Whoy, dudn't ee knaw, Maister Jan," said Bill Dadds, looking at me queerly, "as Jan Vry wur gane afore braxvass ?"

" Oh, very well," I answered, " John knows what he is doing." For John Fry was a kind of foreman now, and it would not do to say anything that would lessen his authority. However I made up my mind to rope him, when I should catch him by himself, without peril to his dignity.

But when I came home in the evening, late and almost weary, there was no Annie cooking my supper, nor Lizzie by the fire reading nor even little Ruth Huckaback watching the shadows and pondering. Upon this, I went to the girls' room, not in the very best of tempers, and there I found the three of them in the little place set apart for Annie, eagerly listening to John Fry, who was telling some great adventure. John had a great jug of ale beside him, and a horn well drained; and he clearly looked upon himself as a hero, and the maids seemed to be of the same opinion.

" Well done, John," my sister was saying, " capitally done, John Fry! How very brave you have been, John! Now quick, let us hear the rest of it."

" What does all this nonsense mean ? " I said angrily. But Annie caught me by the arm and gave me a sweet smile, while little Ruth stood in the doorway.

" Now John, sit down, and you shall know all that we have done, though I doubt whether you will approve of it."

Upon this I kissed Annie and so did Ruth, and John Fry looked a deal more comfortable, but Lizzie only made a face at us. Then Annie began as follows:

" You must know, dear John, that we have been extremely curious, ever since Uncle Reuben came, to know what he was come for, especially at this time of year, when he is at his busiest. If Ruth had known we must have got it out of her before two or three days were over. But she knew no more than we did, indeed she has been quite as inquisitive. Well, we might have put up with it if it had not been for his taking Dolly away every morning, quite as if she belonged to him, and keeping her out until close upon dark, then bringing her home in a frightful condition.

" Then I made John Fry tie her tail in a knot with a piece of white ribbon, as if for adornment, that I might trace her among the hills, at any rate for a mile or two. But Uncle Ben was too deep for that; he cut off the ribbon before he started, saying he would have no Doones after him. And then in despair, I applied to you, knowing how quick of foot you are, and I got Ruth and Lizzie to help me, but you answered us very shortly; and a very poor supper you had that night, according to your deserts.

" But though we were dashed to the ground for a time, we were not wholly discomfited. Our determination to know all about it seemed to increase with the difficulty. And when we came to consider it Ruth was the cleverest of all; for she said that surely we must have some man we could trust, about the farm, to go on a little errand; and then I remembered that old John Fry would do anything for money."

" Not for money, plaize miss," said John Fry, taking a pull at the beer; " but for the love of your swate faice."

" To be sure, John, with the King's behind it. And so Lizzie ran for John Fry at once, and we gave him full directions, how he was to slip out of the barley in the confusion of the breakfast, so that none might miss him; and to run back to the black combe bottom, and there he would find the very same pony which Uncle Ben had been tied upon and there is no faster upon the farm. And then, without waiting for any breakfast, unless he could eat it either running or trotting, he was to travel all up the black combe by the track Uncle Reuben had taken, and up to the top to look forward carefully, and so to trace him without being seen."

" Ay; and raight wull a doo'd un," John cried, with his mouth in the bullock's horn.

" Well, and what did you see, John ? " I asked with great anxiety though I meant to have shown no interest.

" John was just at the very point of it," Lizzie answered me sharply, " when you chose to come in and stop him."

" Then let him begin again," said I. " Things being gone so far, it is my duty to know everything for the sake of you girls and mother."

Therefore John Fry began again. But as he could not tell a tale, I will state in brief what happened.

When John was come to the top of the long black combe, two miles or more from Plover's Barrows, and winding to the southward, he stopped his little nag short of the crest, and got off and looked ahead of him, from behind a stump of whortles. It was a long flat sweep of moorland over which he was gazing, with a few bogs here and there, and bushy places round them. Of course, John Fry from his shepherd life knew the country well. But he could not resist his own great curiosity. For carefully spying across the moor he thought he saw a man on horseback moving in the farthest distance upon Black Barrow Down, making his way very carefully.

John knew that the man who was riding there could be none but Uncle Reuben. Nevertheless, John Fry ached with unbearable curiosity to know what the old man could possibly be after in that mysterious manner.

Therefore he only waited a while for fear of being discovered, till Master Huckabuck turned to the left and entered a little gully, whence he could not survey the moor. Then John remounted and crossed the rough land and the stony places, and picked his way among the morasses, as fast as ever he dared to go; until in about half-an-hour he drew nigh to the entrance to the gully. And now it behoved him to be most wary; for Uncle Ben might have stopped in there. But he soon perceived that the gully was empty. When he had traced the winding hollow for half a mile or more, he saw that it forked, and one part led to the left up a steep red bank, and the other to the right being narrow, and slightly tending downwards.

At last he saw that beyond all doubt the man he was pursuing had taken the course which led down hill; and down the hill he must follow him. But now he knew not where he was, and scarcely dared to ask himself, having heard of a horrible hole, somewhere in this neighbourhood, called the "Wizard's Slough". Therefore John rode down the slope, with sorrow and great caution. Suddenly he turned a corner and saw a scene which stopped him.

For there was the Wizard's Slough itself, as black as death, and bubbling, with a few scant yellow reeds in a ring around it. At the other side of the Slough, and a few land-yards beyond it, where the ground was less noisome, he observed a felled tree over a great hole in the earth, with staves of wood and slabs of stone, and some yellow gravel around it. There he spied Dolly, who seemed not to be harmed by it.

While John was trembling within himself, lest Dolly should get scent of his pony, and neigh and reveal their presence, suddenly to his great amazement, something white arose out of the hole, under the brown trunk of the tree. However, the white thing itself was not so very awful, being nothing more than a long-coned night-cap with a tassel on the top, such as criminals wear at hanging time. But when John saw a man's face under it, and a man's neck and shoulders slowly rising out of the pit, he could not doubt that this was the place where murderers come to life again, according to the Exmoor story.

Therefore he could bear no more, but climbed on his horse with what speed he might, and rode away at full gallop, and after riding hard for an hour, and drinking all his whiskey, he luckily fell in with a shepherd, who led him on to a public-house somewhere near Exford. And he took good care to be home before dark, having followed a well-known sheep-track.

At first I did not believe the story, but was convinced by the honesty of his gaze, when he declared he would not be able to sleep that night.

" I believe you speak the truth, John," I said to him, " and I ask your pardon. Now, not a word to anyone about this strange affair. There is mischief brewing, I can see; and it is my place to attend to it."

Annie pouted and Lizzie frowned, and Ruth looked at me with her eyes wide open, but no further mark of regarding me. And I saw that if any of the three (for John Fry was gone home with the trembles) could be trusted to keep a secret, that one was Ruth Huckaback.

12

LORNA RETURNS JOHN'S LOVE

The story told by John Fry that night, and my conviction of its truth, made me very uneasy, especially as following upon the warning of Judge Jeffreys, and the hints received from Jeremy Stickles, as well as sundry tales and rumours, and signs of secret understanding, seen and heard on market-days, and at places of entertainment. We knew for certain that at Taunton, Bridgewater, and even Dulverton, there was much disaffection towards the King, and regret for the days of the Puritans. Albeit, I had told the truth when I had assured his lordship that to the best of my knowledge there was nothing of the sort with us.

But now I was beginning to doubt whether I might not have been mistaken; especially when we heard, as we did, of arms being landed at Lynmouth in the dead of the night, and of the tramp of men having reached someone's ears, from a hill where a famous echo was. And what better place for this sort of activity than Exmoor ?

But what of Master Huckaback ? Was he likely to have anything to do with rebellion ? What of the Doones ? If anything, they were Catholics, but desperate men like these might make common cause with the Protestants in any uprising, especially as they would hardly feel any loyalty to the son of the man who had outlawed them. But before I had time to ponder much on these problems, Uncle Ben went away, as suddenly as he first had come to us, giving no reason for his departure, but leaving little Ruth with us.

By this time, the harvest being done, I began to burn in spirit for the sight of Lorna again, having meantime begged my sister Annie to let Sally Snowe know, once and for all, that it was not in my power to have anything more to do with her.

Inasmuch as there are two sorts of month well recognized by the calendar, to wit the lunar and the solar, I made bold to regard both my months, in the absence of any provision, as intended to be strictly lunar. Therefore, upon the very day when the eight weeks were expiring, forth I went in search of Lorna, taking the pearl ring hopefully, and all the new-laid eggs I could find, and a dozen and a half of small trout from our brook.

But alas, I was utterly disappointed; for although I waited and waited for hours, with an equal amount both of patience and peril, no Lorna ever appeared at all, nor even the faintest sign of her. And another thing occurred as well, which vexed me more than it need have done, for so small a matter. And this was that my little offering of the trout, and the new-laid eggs, was carried off in the coolest manner by that vile Carver Doone, who happened to be wandering about in that part of the valley. I promptly hid in a drain, having no arms to defend myself, until he went off.

Having waited until there was no chance whatever of my love appearing, I hastened homeward very sadly. Nevertheless, I went every evening, thenceforward for a fortnight; hoping every time in vain to find my hope and comfort. And meanwhile what perplexed me most was that the signals were replaced, in order as agreed upon, so that Lorna could scarcely be restrained by any rigour.

To tell the truth, I was heartily tired of lurking and playing bo-peep so long; to which nothing could have reconciled me, except my fear for Lorna. And growing more and more uneasy, as I found no Lorna, I would have tried to force the Doone Glen from the upper end, and take my chance of getting back, but for Annie and her prayers.

Now that same night, I think it was, or at any rate the next one, I noticed Betty Muxworthy going on most strangely. She made the queerest signs to me when nobody was looking, and laid her fingers on her lips, and pointed over her shoulder. But I took little heed of her, being in a kind of dudgeon, and oppressed with evil luck; believing too, that all she wanted was to have some little grumble about some petty grievance.

But presently she poked me with the heel of a fire-bundle, and passing close to my ear whispered, so that none else could hear her: " Larna Doo-un."

By these words I was so startled, that I turned round and stared at her; but she pretended not to know it, and began with all her might to scour an empty crock with a besom.

" Oh, Betty, let me help you! That work is much too hard for you," I cried with a sudden chivalry, which only won rude answer.

" Zeed me a-dooing of thic, every naight last ten year, Jan, wiout vindin' out how hard it wor. But if zo bee thee wants to help, carr pegs' bucket for me. Massy, if I aint forgotten to fade the pegs till now."

Favouring me with another wink, to which I now paid the keenest heed, Betty went and fetched the lanthorn from the hook inside the door. Then when she had kindled it, not allowing me any time to ask what she was after, she went outside and pointed to the great bock of wash, saying to me quietly as a maiden might ask one to carry a glove, " Jan Ridd, car thic thing for me."

So I carried it for her, without any words. And when we came to hog-pound, she turned upon me suddenly with the lanthorn she was bearing, and saw that I had the bock by one hand very easily.

" Jan Ridd," she said, " there be no other man in England cud a'dood it. Now thee shalt have Larna."

While I was wondering how my chance of having Lorna could depend upon my power to carry pigs' wash, I saw that Betty would not tell me another word, until all the pigs were served. When this was done she said quietly: " Hould thee head down same as they pegs do."

So I bent my head quite close to her; and she whispered into my ear, " Goo of a marning, thee girt soft. Her can't get out of an avening now, her hath sent word to me, to tull 'ee."

Of course I was up the very next morning before the October sunrise, and away up to the Doone Valley. But the sun was beginning to glisten over the comb of the Eastern highland, when, much abashed with joy, I saw Lorna coming.

" At last then, you are come, John; I thought you had forgotten me. I could not make you understand—they have kept me prisoner every evening: but come into my house; you are in danger here."

Meanwhile, I could not answer, being overcome with joy; but followed to her little grotto, where I had been twice before. I knew that the crowning moment of my life was coming—that Lorna would own her love for me.

She made for a while as if she dreamed not of the meaning of my gaze, but tried to speak of other things, faltering now and then, and mantling with a richer damask below her long lashes.

" This is not what I came to know " I whispered very softly; " you know what I am come to ask."

" If you are come on purpose to ask anything, why do you delay so ? " She turned away very bravely, but I saw that her lips were trembling.

" I delay so long, because I fear; because my whole life hangs in balance on a single word; because what I have near me now may never more be near me after, though more than all the world, or than a thousand worlds, to me." As I spoke these words of passion in a low soft voice, Lorna trembled more and more; but she made no answer, neither yet looked up at me.

"I have loved you long and long," I pursued, being reckless now; "when a little child, as a boy I worshipped you; then when I saw you a comely girl, as a stripling I adored you; now that you are a full-grown maiden, all the rest I do and more—I love you more than tongue can tell, or heart can hold in silence. I have waited long and long; and though I am so far below you, I can wait no longer; but must have my answer."

"You have been very faithful, John," she murmured to the fern and moss; "I suppose I must reward you."

"That will not do for me," I said, "I will not have reluctant liking, nor assent for pity's sake; which only means endurance. I must have all love or none; I must have your heart of hearts; even as you have mine, Lorna."

While I spoke she glanced up shyly, through her fluttering lashes, to prolong my doubt one moment, for her own delicious pride. Then she opened wide upon me all the glorious depths and softness of her loving eyes, and flung both arms around my neck, and answered with her heart on mine:

"Darling, you have won it all. I shall never be my own again. I am yours, my own one, for ever and ever."

I am sure I know not what I did or what I said thereafter. Only one thing I remember, when she raised her bright lips to me like a child for me to kiss, such a smile of sweet temptation met me through her flowing hair, that I almost forgot my manners, giving her no time to breathe.

"That will do," said Lorna gently, but violently blushing; "for the present that will do, John. And now remember one thing, dear. All the kindness is to be on my side; and you are to be very distant, as behoves to a young maiden; oh yes! you may kiss my hand, you know! Ah, to be sure! I had forgotten; how very stupid of me!"

For by this I had taken one sweet hand and gazed on it, with the pride of all the world to think that such a lovely thing was mine; and then I slipped my little ring upon the wedding finger; and this time Lorna kept it, and looked with fondness on its beauty, and clung to me with a flood of tears.

"Every time you cry," said I, drawing her closer to me, "I shall consider it an invitation to be not too distant. There now, none shall make you weep. Darling, you shall sigh no more, but live in peace and happiness, with me to guard and cherish you; and who shall dare to vex you?" But she drew a long sad sigh, and looked at the ground with the great tears rolling, and pressed one hand upon the trouble of her pure, young breast.

"It can never, never be," she murmured to herself alone. "Who am I to dream of it? Something in my heart tells me, it can be so never, never."

There was, however, no possibility of depressing me at such a time. To be loved by Lorna, the fairest creature on God's earth, and the most enchanting, the lady of high birth and mind; that I, a mere clumsy, blundering yeoman, without wit, or wealth or lineage, should have won that loving heart to be my own for ever, was a thought no fears could lessen, and no chance could steal from me.

Therefore, at her own entreaty taking a very quick adieu, and by her own invitation an exceeding kind one, I hurried home with deep exulting, yet some sad misgivings, for Lorna had made me promise now to tell my mother everything.

Unluckily for my designs, who should be sitting down at breakfast with my mother and the rest but Squire Faggus, as everybody now began to entitle him. I noticed something uncomfortable in his manner, and a lack of his usual ease and humour, which had been wont to distinguish him.

Later, when I returned from the furrows, Squire Faggus was gone and Lizzie came running to meet me, at the bottom of the wood-rick and cried:

"Oh, John, mother is in such a state of mind, and Annie crying her eyes out. What do you think? You never would guess; though I have suspected it, ever so long."

"No need for me to guess," I replied, as though with

some indifference, because of her self-important air; " I knew all about it long ago. You have not been crying much, I see. I should like you better if you had."

" Why should I cry ? I like Tom Faggus. He is the only one I ever see with the spirit of a man."

We entered the house together; and mother sent at once for me, while I was trying to console my darling sister Annie.

" Oh, John! Speak one good word for me," she cried with both hands laid in mine, and her tearful eyes looking up at me.

" Not one, my pet, but a hundred," I answered kindly, embracing her; " have no fear, little sister; I am going to make your case so bright, by comparision, I mean, that mother will send for you in five minutes, and call you her best her most dutiful child and praise cousin Tom to the skies, and send a man on horseback after him; and then you will have a harder task to intercede for me, my dear."

" Oh, John, dear John, you won't tell her about Lorna— oh, not today, dear."

" Yes, today and at once Annie. I want to have it over and be done with it."

" Oh, but think of her, dear. I am sure she could not bear it, after this great shock already."

" She will bear it all the better," said I; " the one will drive the other out."

Now inasmuch as the thing befell, according to my prediction, what need for me to dwell upon it, after saying how it would be ? By the afternoon, when the sun began to go down upon us, our mother sat on the garden bench, with her head on my great otter-skin waistcoat (which was waterproof) and her right arm round our Annie's waist, and scarcely knowing which of us she ought to make the most of, or which deserved most pity. Not that she had forgiven yet the rivals to her love—Tom Faggus, I mean, and Lorna—but that she was beginning to think a little better of them now, and a vast deal better of her own children.

Mother was full of plans after that to bring Lorna to

Plover's Barrows, but alas, they were not practicable. Unfortunately too, she raised her voice in anger against Master Huckaback and his dwarf of a granddaughter, and little Ruth, having overheard her remarks, returned to Dulverton next day in high dudgeon.

After this I found it needful, according to the strictest good sense and honour, to visit Lorna, immediately after my discourse with mother, and to tell her all about it. My beauty gave me one sweet kiss with all her heart (as she always did, when she kissed at all), and I begged for one more to take to our mother, and before leaving I obtained it. It is not for me to tell all she said, except this, which I carried word for word, to my mother and Annie:

" I can never believe, dear John, that after all the crime and outrage wrought by my reckless family, it ever can be meant for me to settle down to peace and comfort in a simple household. With all my heart I long for home; any home, however dull and wearisome to those used to it, would seem a paradise to me, if only free from brawl and tumult, and such as I could call my own. But even if God would allow me this, in lieu of my wild inheritance, it is quite certain that the Doones never can, and never will."

Again, when I told her how my mother and Annie, as well as myself, longed to have her at Plover's Barrows, and teach her all the quiet duties in which she was sure to take such delight, she only answered with a bright blush, that while her grandfather was living, she would never leave him. She then asked how long I would wait for her.

" Not a day, if I had my will," I answered very warmly; at which she turned away confused, and would not look at me for a while; " but all my life," I went on to say, " if my fortune is so ill. And how long would you wait for me, Lorna ? "

" Till I could get you," she answered slily, with a smile which was brighter to me than the brightest wit could be. " And now " she continued, " you bound me, John, with a very beautiful ring to you, and when I dare not wear it, I carry it always on my heart. But I will bind you to me, you dearest, with the very poorest and plainest thing that ever you set eyes on. I could give you fifty fairer ones but they would not be honest; and I love you for your honesty, and nothing else of course, John, so don't you be conceited. Look at it, what a queer old thing! There are some ancient marks upon it, very grotesque and wonderful; it looks like a cat in a tree, almost, but never mind what it looks like. This old ring must have been a giant's, therefore it will fit you, perhaps, you enormous John. It has been on the front of my old glass necklace—the one I wore from childhood and which grandfather now keeps for me because the others wanted it. He left me the ring to wear on a thread round my neck. Now you seem very greatly amazed; pray, what thinks my lord of it? "

" That is worth fifty of the pearl thing I gave you, you darling. This is not the ring of any giant. It is nothing more nor less than a very ancient thumb-ring, such as once in my father's time was ploughed up out of the ground in our farm, and sent to learned doctors, who told us all about it but kept the ring for their trouble. I will accept it, my own one love."

All this, or at least great part of it, I told my mother truly, according to my promise; and she was greatly pleased with Lorna for having been so good to me, and for speaking so very sensibly, and then she looked at the great gold ring, but could by no means interpret. Only she was quite certain, as indeed as I myself was, that it must have belonged to an ancient race of great consideration and high rank, in their time.

And before I got used to my ring, or people could think that it belonged to me, and before I went to see Lorna again, having failed to find any necessity, and remembering my duty to mother, we all had something else to think of, not so pleasant, and even more puzzling.

13

A VERY DESPERATE VENTURE

Now November was upon us, and while we were at wheat sowing, another visitor arrived. This was Master Jeremy Stickles, who had been a good friend to me in London, and earned my mother's gratitude. He made our farmhouse his headquarters, and kept us quite at his beck and call. He was on the King's service, had troopers at his command and was always armed. One day he took me aside.

" John," he said, " you have some right to know the meaning of all this, being trusted as you were by the Lord Chief Justice. But he found you scarcely supple enough, neither gifted with due brains."

" Thank God for that same," I answered, while he tapped his head to signify his own much larger allowance. Then he made me bind myself, which in an evil hour I did, to retain his secret; and after that he went on solemnly and with much importance:

" There be some people fit to plot, and others to be plotted against, and others to unravel plots, which is the highest gift of all. This last hath fallen to my share, and a very thankless gift it is, although a rare and choice one. Now, heard you much in London town about the Duke of Monmouth ? "

" Not so very much," I answered; " not half so much as in Devonshire; only that he was a hearty man and a very handsome one, and now was banished by the Tories; and most people wished he was coming back instead of the Duke of York."

" Things have changed since you were in town. The Whigs are getting up again, and having been punished bitterly for the blood they shed, are ripe for any violence. And the turn of the balance is now to them. See-saw is the fashion of England always; and the Whigs will soon be the top-sawyers. Now in ten words (without parties, or trying thy poor brain too much), I am here to watch the gathering of a secret plot, not so much against the King as against the due succession. Now hearken to one who wishes thee well, and plainly sees the end of it—stick thou to the winning side, and have nought to do with the other one."

"That," said I, in great haste and hurry, "is the very thing I want to do, if I only knew which was the winning side, for the sake of Lorna—that is to say, for the sake of my dear mother and sisters, and the farm."

"Ha!" cried Jeremy Stickles, laughing at the redness of my face, "Lorna, saidst thou; now what Lorna? Is it the name of a maiden or a light-o'-love?"

"Keep to your business," I answered very proudly and caused him grave offence for a long time afterwards.

But now my own affairs were thrown into such disorder, that I could think of nothing else, and had the greatest difficulty in hiding my uneasiness; for suddenly all my Lorna's signals ceased.

Three times I went to look; but though I waited at every hour of day and far into the night, no light footstep came to meet me, no sweet voice was in the air; all was lonely, drear and drenched with sodden desolation.

Once I sought far up the valley, where I had never been before, even beyond the copse, where Lorna had found and lost her brave young cousin. Following up the river channel in the shelter of the evening fog, I gained a corner within stone's throw of the last outlying cot; for knowing it to be Carver's dwelling, I was led by curiosity to have a closer look at it. I found it empty. It was well for me that I did this, as you will find hereafter.

Before I took myself home that night, and eased dear mother's heart so much, and made her sad face spread with smiles, I had resolved to penetrate Glen Doone from the upper end, and learn all about my Lorna.

The journey was a great deal longer to fetch around the southern hills, and enter by the Doone-gate, than to cross the lower land, and steal in by the water-slide. Slowly, however, I came to the robbers' highway, but I thought it safer to wait a little, as twilight melted into night; and then I crept down a seam of the highland, and stood upon the Doone track.

As the road approached the entrance, it became more straight and strong, like a channel cut from rock, with the water brawling darkly along the naked side of it. Not a tree or bush was left to shelter a man from bullets; all was stern, and stiff and rugged.

And here I was, or seemed to be, particularly unlucky; for as I drew near the entrance, lightly of foot and warily, the moon broke upon me, topping the eastward ridge of rock and filling all the open spaces with the play of wavering light. I shrank back into the shadowy quarter, on the right side of the road; and gloomily employed myself to watch the triple entrance, on which the moonlight fell askew.

Now I could see those three rough arches, jagged, black and terrible; and I knew that only one of them could lead me to the valley; neither gave the river now any further guidance, but dived underground with a sullen roar, where it met the cross-bar of the mountain. Having no means at all of judging which was the right way of the three, I was puzzled, but after some thought it struck me that, in times of peace, the middle way was the likeliest.

Therefore, without more hesitation, I plunged into the middle way, holding a long ash staff before me, shodden at the end with iron. In black darkness, groping along the wall, I nearly blundered full upon the sentries. As it was I had barely time to draw back, as I turned a corner upon them.

There seemed to be only two of them, of size indeed and stature as all the Doones must be, but I need not have feared to encounter them both, had they been unarmed as I was. They were drinking and not very sober and I paused to watch them. At length, weary of waiting, I feigned the call of an owl, and slipped past them as they peered round to see where the large night bird was. I came out in the top of the meadowland and had fair view and outline of the robbers' township, spread with bushes here and there, but not heavily overshadowed. The moon, approaching now the full, brought the forms in manner forth, clothing each with character, as the moon (more than the sun) does, to an eye accustomed.

I knew that the Captain's house was first, both from what Lorna had said of it, and from my mother's description, and keeping as much as possible in the shadows, I crept up to a window higher than the rest above the ground and with a faint light moving. This could hardly fail to be the room wherein my darling lay. Fortunately the sentinel on the west, challenging me, took me for Carver Doone. Thinking Carver wished to have some private talk with Lorna and not caring to disturb him, he did not follow up his challenge, but withdrew discreetly.

Meanwhile he had done me the kindest service, for Lorna came to the window at once, to see what the cause of the shout was, and drew back the curtain timidly. Then she opened the rough lattice and watched the cliff and trees; then she sighed very sadly.

" Oh, Lorna, don't you know me ? " I whispered from the side, being afraid of startling her by appearing over suddenly.

Quick though she always was of thought, she knew me not from my whisper, and was shutting the window hastily, when I caught it back and showed myself.,

" John! " she cried, yet with sense enough not to speak aloud: " oh, you must be mad, John."

" As mad as a March hare," said I, " without any news of my darling. You knew I would come, of course you did."

" Well, I thought, perhaps—you know: now, John, you need not eat my hand. Do you see they have put iron bars across ? "

" To be sure. Do you think I should be contented, even with this lovely hand, but for these vile iron bars ? I will have them out before I go. Now, darling, for one moment— just the other hand, for a change, you know."

So I got the other, but was not honest; for I kept them both and felt their delicate beauty trembling, as I laid them to my heart.

" Oh, John, you will make me cry directly "—she had been crying long ago—" if you go on in that way. You know we can never have one another; everyone is against it. Why should I make you miserable? Try not to think of me any more."

" And will you try the same of me, Lorna? "

" Oh, yes, John; if you agree to it. At least I will try to try it."

" Then you won't try anything of the sort," I cried with great enthusiasm, for her tone was so nice and melancholy: " the only thing we will try to try, is to belong to one another. And if we do our best, Lorna, God alone can prevent us."

She crossed herself, with one hand drawn free, as I spoke so boldly; and something swelled in her little throat, and prevented her from answering.

" Now tell me," I said, " what means all this? Why are you so pent up here? Why have you given me no token? Has your grandfather turned against you? Are you in any danger? "

" My poor grandfather is very ill: I fear that he will not live long. The Counsellor and his son are now the masters of the valley; and I dare not venture forth, for fear of anything they might do to me. When I went forth to signal you, Carver tried to seize me; but I was too quick for him. Little Gwenny is not allowed to leave they valley now; so that I could send no message. I have been so wretched, dear, lest you should think me false to you. The tyrants now make sure of me. You must watch this house, both night and day, if you wish to save me. There is nothing they would shrink from, if my poor grandfather—oh, I cannot bear to think of myself, when I ought to think of him only; dying without a son to tend him or a daughter to shed a tear."

" But surely he has sons enough; why do none of them come to him? "

" I know not. I cannot tell. He is a very strange old man; and few have ever loved him. He was black with wrath at the Counsellor, this very afternoon—but I must not keep you here—you are much too brave, John; and I am much too selfish: there, what was that shadow ? "

" Nothing more than a bat, darling, come to look for his sweetheart. I will not stay long; you tremble so; and yet for that very reason, how can I leave you, Lorna ? "

" You must—you must," she answered. " I shall die if they hurt you. I hear the old nurse moving. Grandfather is sure to send for me. Keep back from the window."

However, it was only Gwenny Carfax, Lorna's little hand-maid; my darling brought her to the window, and presented her to me, almost laughing through her grief.

" Oh, I am so glad, John; Gwenny, I am so glad you came. It is rather dark, but you can see him. I wish you to know him again, Gwenny."

" Whoy! " cried Gwenny, with great amazement, standing on tiptoe to look out, and staring as if she were weighing me: " her be bigger than any Doone. Heared as her have bate our Carnish champion awrastling. 'Twadn't fair play nohow; no, no, don't tell me, 'twadn't fair play nohow."

" True enough, Gwenny," I answered her; for the play had been very unfair indeed on the side of the Bodmin champion: " it was not a fair bout, little maid; I am free to acknowledge that." By that answer, or rather by the con-struction she put upon it, the heart of the Cornish girl was won, more than by gold or silver.

" I shall knoo thee again, young man, no fear of that," she answered, nodding with an air of patronage. " Now, Missie, gae on courtin', and I will gae outside and watch for ee." I was very thankful to Gwenny for taking her departure.

" She is the best little thing in the world," said Lorna, softly laughing; " and the queerest, and the truest. Nothing will bribe her against me. If she seems to be on the other side, never, never doubt her. Now no more of your 'coortin', John! I love you far too well for that. Yes, yes, ever so much! And much as ever you like to imagine; and then you may double it after that. Only go, do go, good John; kind, dear, darling John; if you love me, go."

"How can I go without settling anything?" I asked, very sensibly. "How shall I know of your danger now? Hit upon something, you are so quick. Anything you can think of, and then I will go, and not frighten you."

"I have been thinking long of something," Lorna answered rapidly, with that peculiar clearness of voice which made every syllable ring like music of a several note. "You see that tree with the seven rooks' nests, bright against the cliffs there. Can you count them from above, do you think? From a place where you will be safe, dear. . . ."

"No doubt I can; or if I cannot, it will not take me long to find a spot whence I can do it."

"Gwenny can climb like any cat. She has been up there in the summer, watching the young birds, day by day, and daring the boys to touch them. There are neither birds nor eggs there now, of course, and nothing doing. If you see but six rooks' nests, I am in peril and want you. If you see but five, I am carried off by Carver."

"Good heavens!" said I at the mere idea, in a tone which frightened Lorna.

"Fear not, John," she whispered sadly, and my blood grew cold at it: "I have means to stop him; or at least to save myself. If you can come within one day of that man's getting hold of me, you will find me quite unharmed. After that, you will find me dead, or alive, according to circumstances."

Her dear, sweet face was full of pride, as even in the gloom I saw. I only said, "God bless you, darling!" and she said the same to me, in a very low sad voice. And then I stole away.

A weight of care was off my mind; though much of trouble hung there still. One thing was quite certain—if Lorna could not have John Ridd, no one else should have her. And my mother, who sat up for me, and with me long time afterwards, agreed that this was comfort.

14

A GOOD TURN FOR JEREMY

John Fry had now six shillings a week of regular and permanent wage, besides all harvest and shearing money, as well as a cottage rent free, and enough of garden ground to rear pot-herbs for his wife and all his family. Now the wages appointed by our Justices, at the time of sessions, were four and sixpence a week for summer and a shilling less for the winter time; and we could be fined and perhaps imprisoned, for giving more than the sums so fixed. Therefore John Fry was looked upon as the richest labourer upon Exmoor, but there was no more discontented man, more sure that he had not his worth, neither half so sore about it, than, or as, John Fry. And he regularly threatened to lay information against us for paying him too much wages! Without this flaw in his character there was no explaining John's dealings with Jeremy Stickles.

Ever since I had offended Jeremy, by threatening him in case of his meddling with my personal affairs, he had more and more allied himself with simple-minded John, as he was pleased to call him.

It appears that John related, for a certain consideration, all that he had seen at Wizard's Slough, and doubtless more which had accrued to it. Upon this Master Stickles was most astonished at Uncle Reuben's proceedings, having always accounted him a most loyal, keen and wary subject.

All this I learned upon recovering Jeremy's good graces, which came to pass in no other way than by the saving of his life. Being bound to keep the strictest watch upon the seven rooks' nests, and yet not bearing to be idle and to waste my mother's stores, I contrived to keep my work entirely at the western corner of our farm, which was nearest to Glen Doone, and whence I could easily run to a height commanding the view I coveted.

One day, Squire Faggus had dropped in upon us just in time for dinner and very soon he and the King's messenger were as thick as need be. Tom had brought his beloved mare to show her off to Annie, and was in great spirits having just accomplished a purchase of land which was worth ten times what he gave for it. It was clear that I was not wanted.

Therefore I strode away up the lane to my afternoon's employment and worked very hard in the copse of young ash, with my bill-hook and a shearing knife. It is not to be supposed that I did all this work, without many peeps at the seven rooks'. nests, which proved my Lorna's safety. Indeed, whenever I wanted a change, I was up and away to the ridge of the hill, instead of standing and doing nothing.

When it was time to go home to supper, I wiped my bill-hook and shearing knife very carefully, for I hate to leave tools dirty; and was doubting whether I should try for another glance at the seven rooks' nests, or whether it would be too dark for it. It was now a quarter of an hour mayhap, since I had made any chopping noise; to this, no doubt, I owe my life, which then (without my dreaming it) was in no little jeopardy.

For just as I was twisting the bine of my very last faggot, before tucking the cleft tongue under, there came three men outside the hedge, where the western light was yellow, and by it I could see that all three of them carried fire-arms. These men were not walking carelessly, but following down the hedge-trough, as if to stalk some enemy. With a sort of instinct I threw myself flat in among the thick fern, and held my breath and lay still as a log. Then the three men came to the gap in the hedge, where I had been in and out so often; and stood up and looked in over.

" Somebody's been at work here "—it was the deep voice of Carver Doone; " jump up Charlie and look about; we must have no witnesses."

" Give me a hand behind," said Charlesworth Doone, " this bank is too devilish steep for me."

" Nonsense, man! " said Marwood de Whichehalse, who,

to my amazement, was the third of the number. "Only a hind cutting faggots; and of course he hath gone home long ago."

At that I drew my breath again, and thanked God I had gotten my coat on.

"There is a big young fellow upon this farm," Carver Doone muttered sulkily, "with whom I have an account to settle, if ever I come across him. He hath a cursed spite to us, because we shot his father. He was going to bring the lumpers upon us, only he was afeared, last winter. And he hath been in London lately, for some traitorous job, no doubt."

"Oh, you mean that fool, John Ridd," answered the young squire. "A very simple clod-hopper. No treachery in him, I warrant; he hath not the head for it. All he cares about is wrestling. As strong as a bull and with no more brains."

"A bullet for that bull," said Carver; and I could see the grin on his scornful face; "a bullet for ballast to his brain, the first time I come across him."

"Nonsense, captain! I won't have him shot, for he is my old school-fellow and hath a very pretty sister. But his cousin is of a different mould, and ten times as dangerous."

"We shall see, lads, we shall see," grumbled the great blackbearded man. "Ill bodes for the fool that would hinder me. But come, let us onward. No lingering or the viper will be in the bush from us. Body and soul, if he give us the slip, both of you shall answer it."

"No fear, captain, and no hurry," Charlie answered gallantly; "would I were as sure of living a twelvemonth as he is of dying within the hour! Extreme unction for him in my bullet patch. Remember I claim to be his confessor, because he hath insulted me."

"Thou art welcome to the job for me," said Marwood, as they turned away, and kept along the hedge-row. "I love to meet a man sword to sword; not to pop at him from a foxhole."

What answer was made, I could not hear, but my curiosity

was so much aroused that I followed them down the fence, as gently as a rabbit goes, only I was inside it and they on the outside; but yet so near that I heard the branches rustle as they pushed them.

"We shall see him better in there," said Carver in his horrible gruff voice, like the creaking of the gallows chain; "sit there, behind holly hedge, lads, while he cometh down yonder hill; and then our good evening to him; one at his body and two at his head, and good aim, lest we baulk the devil."

"I tell you, captain, that will not do," said Charlie, almost whispering: "you are very proud of your skill, we know, and can hit a lark if you see it: but he may not come until after dark, and we cannot be too nigh him. This holly hedge is too far away. He crosses down here from Slocombeslade, not from Tibbacot, I tell you; but along that track to the left there, and so by the foreland to Glenthorne, where his boat is in the cove.. Do you think I have tracked him so many evenings, without knowing his line to a hair? Will you fool away all my trouble?"

"Come then, lad, we will follow your lead. Thy life for his, if we fail of it."

"After me, then, right into the hollow; thy legs are growing stiff, captain."

"So shall thy body be, young man, if thou leadest me astray in this."

I heard them stumbling down the hill, which was steep and rocky in that part; and peering through the hedge, I saw them enter a covert, by the side of the track which Master Stickles followed, almost every evening, when he left our house upon business. And then I knew who it was they had come on purpose to murder—a thing which I might have guessed long before, but for terror and cold stupidity.

It seemed to me that my only chance to stop the mischief pending was to compass the round of the hill, as fast as feet could be laid to ground; so as to stop the King's messenger from travelling any farther, if only I could catch him there.

And this was exactly what I did; and a terrible run I had for it, fearing at every step to hear the echo of the shots in the valley.

"Jeremy, Jerry," was all I could say, being so fearfully short of breath; for I had crossed the ground quicker than any horse could.

"Spoken just in time, John Ridd!" cried Master Stickles, still pointing a great horse-pistol at me. "I might have known thee by thy size, John. What art doing here?"

"Come to save your life. For God's sake go no farther. Three men in the covert there, with long guns, waiting for thee."

"Ha! I have been watched of late. That is why I pointed at thee, John. Back round this corner and get thy breath, and tell me all about it. I never saw a man so hurried. I could beat thee now, John."

Jeremy Stickles was a man of courage and presence of mind; nevertheless he trembled greatly, when he heard what I had to tell him. But I took good care to keep back the name of young Marwood de Whichehalse; neither did I show my knowledge of the other men, for reasons of my own not very hard to conjecture.

"We will let them cool their heels, John Ridd," said Jeremy after thinking a little. "I cannot fetch my musketeers from Glenthorne or Lynmouth, in time to seize the fellows. One result this attempt will have, good John, it will make me thy friend for ever. Shake hands, my lad, and forgive me freely for having been so cold to thee. Mayhap in the troubles coming, it will help thee not a little to have done me this good turn."

Stickles took me aside the next day, and opened all his business to me, whether I would or not. Disaffection to the King, or rather, dislike to his brother James, and fear of Roman ascendancy, had existed now for several years and of late were spreading rapidly, especially in places like Taunton, Bridgewater, Minehead and Dulverton. This was due partly to other causes, partly that natural tide in all political channels, which verily moves as if it had the moon itself for its mistress. As a Tory watchman, or spy, as the Whigs would call him, Jeremy Stickles was now among us; and his duty was threefold.

First, and most ostensibly, to see to the levying of poundage in the little haven of Lynmouth, and further up the coast, which was now becoming a place of resort for the folk whom we call smugglers.

Second, his duty (though only the Doones had discovered it) to watch and report on those outlaws.

Jeremy Stickles' third business was entirely political; to learn the temper of our people and the gentle families, to watch the movements of the trained bands (which could not always be trusted), to discover any collecting of arms and drilling of men among us, to prevent any importation of gunpowder, in a word, to observe and forestall the enemy.

To the surprise of Jeremy, I would have nothing to do with the attack on the Doones. I assured him it was not from any lack of loyalty; but I feared for the safety of my own beloved Lorna, and in any case, we had had a magnificent harvest, and with all these troubles brewing, perhaps every sheaf in our own yard was destined to be burned or stolen, before we had finished the bread we had baked.

Among all these troubles, there seemed to be one comfort. Tom Faggus returned from London very proudly and very happily, with a royal pardon in black and white, which everybody admired the more, because no one could read a word of it.

15

TWO FOOLS TOGETHER

When I went up one morning to look for my seven rooks' nests, behold there were but six to be seen. The signal was made for me to come, because my love was in danger. For me to enter the valley now, during broad daylight, could have brought no comfort, but only harm to the maiden, and certain death to myself. Yet it was more than I could do to keep altogether at distance; therefore I ran to the nearest place where I could remain unseen, and watched the glen from the wooded height for hours and hours impatiently with nothing I cared to do, except blow on my fingers and long for more wit.

For a frost was beginning, which made a great difference to Lorna and to myself, I trow; as well as to all the five million people who dwell in this island of England; such a frost as never I saw before,* neither hope ever to see again; a time when it was impossible to milk a cow for icicles, or for a man to shave some of his beard (as I liked to do for Lorna's sake, because she was so smooth) without blunting his razor on hard grey ice. No man could " keep yatt " (as we say) even though he abandoned his work altogether, and thumped himself all on the chest and front, till his frozen hands would have been bleeding except for the cold that kept still all his veins.

It was lucky for me, while I waited here, that our very best sheep-dog, old Watch, had chosen to accompany me that day. When it grew towards dark, I was just beginning to prepare for my circuit round the hills; but suddenly Watch gave a long, low growl; I kept myself close as possible and ordered the dog to be silent, and presently a short figure approached from a thickly wooded hollow on the left side of my hiding-place. It was the same figure I had seen once before in the moonlight, at Plover's Barrows; and proved to my great delight, to be the little maid Gwenny Carfax. She started a moment, at seeing me, but more with surprise than fear; and then she laid both her hands upon mine, as if she had known me for twenty years.

*If John Ridd lived until the year 1740 (as so strong a man was bound to do) he must have seen almost a harder frost; and perhaps it put an end to him; for then he would be some four-score years old. But tradition makes him " keep yatt ", as he says, up to five score years.—Ed.L.D.

"Young man," she said, "you must come with me. I was gwain all the way to fetch thee. Old man be dying; and her can't die, or at least, her won't without first considering thee."

"Considering me!" I cried. "What can Sir Ensor Doone want with considering me? Has Mistress Lorna told him?"

"All concerning thee and thy doings; when she knowed old man were so near his end. That vexed he was about thy low blood, a' thought her would come to life again, on purpose for to bate 'ee. But after all, there can't be scarcely such bad luck as that."

With great misgiving of myself, but no ill thought of my darling, I sent Watch home, and followed Gwenny to the top of Doone valley. In the chilly dusk air it looked most untempting, especially during that state of mind under which I was labouring. As we crossed towards the Captain's house, a couple of great Doones let me pass without hindrance. It is not too much to say that, when the little maid opened Sir Ensor's door, my heart thumped quite as much with terror as with hope of Lorna's presence.

But in a moment the fear was gone, for Lorna was trembling in my arms, and my courage rose to comfort her. The darling feared, beyond all things else, lest I should be offended with her, for what she had said to her grandfather, and for dragging me into his presence; but I told her that I cared not that much for old Sir Ensor and all his wrath, so long as I had his granddaughter's love.

But Lorna took me by the hand as bravely as she could, and led me into a little passage, where I could hear the river moaning and the branches rustling.

Here I passed as long a minute as fear ever cheated time of. At last my Lorna came back very pale, as I saw by the candle she carried, and whispered: "Now be patient, dearest. Never mind what he says to you; neither attempt to answer him. Look at him gently and steadfastly, and, if you can, with some show of reverence; but above all things, no compassion; it drives him almost mad. Now come, and walk very quietly."

She led me into a cold, dark room, rough and very gloomy, although with two candles burning. That which I heeded was an old man, very stern and comely, with death upon his countenance; yet not lying in his bed, but set upright in a chair, with a loose red cloak thrown over him. Upon this his white hair fell, and his pale fingers lay in a ghastly fashion, without a sign of life or movement or of the power that kept him up; all rigid, calm and relentless. Only in his great black eyes, fixed upon me solemnly, all the power of his body dwelt, all the life of his soul was burning. I made a low obeisance, and tried not to shiver. Only I groaned that Lorna thought it good manners to leave us two together.

"Ah," said the old man, and his voice seemed to come from a cavern of skeletons; "are you that great John Ridd?"

"John Ridd is my name, your honour," was all that I could answer, "and I hope your worship is better."

"Child, have you sense enough to know what you have been doing?"

"Yes, I know right well," I answered, "that I have set mine eyes far above my rank."

"Are you ignorant that Lorna Doone is born of the oldest families remaining in North Europe?"

"I was ignorant of that, your worship; yet I knew of her high descent from the Doones of Bagworthy."

The old man's eyes, like fire, probed me whether I was jesting; then perceiving how grave I was, and thinking that I could not laugh (as many people suppose of me), he took on himself to make good the deficiency with a very bitter smile.

"And know you of your own low descent, from the Ridds of Oare?"

"Sir," I answered, being as yet unaccustomed to this style of speech, "the Ridds of Oare have been honest men, twice as long as the Doones have been rogues."

"I would not answer for that, John," Sir Ensor replied

very quietly, when I expected fury. " If it be so, thy family is the very oldest in Europe. Now hearken to an old man's words who has not many hours to live. There is nothing in this world to fear, nothing to revere or trust, nothing even to hope for; least of all, is there ought to love."

" I hope your worship is not quite right," I answered with great misgivings; " else it is a mistake for anybody to live sad, sir."

" Therefore," he continued, as if I had never spoken, " though it may seem hard for a week or two, like the loss of any other toy, I deprive you of nothing but add to your comfort and to your happiness, when I forbid you ever to see that foolish child again. You will pledge your word in Lorna's presence, never to see or to seek her again; never even to think of her more. Now call her, for I am weary."

I found that my love (or not my love, according as how she should behave; for I was very desperate, being put upon so sadly) Lorna Doone was crying softly at a little window, and listening to the river's grief. I laid my heavy arm around her and to my heart, once for all, she spoke with her own upon it. Not a word, nor sound between us; not even a kiss was interchanged; but man, or maid, who has ever loved hath learned our understanding.

Therefore it came to pass, that we saw fit to enter Sir Ensor's room in the following manner. Lorna, with her right hand swallowed entirely by the palm of mine, and her waist retired from view by means of my left arm. All one side of her hair came down, in a way to be remembered upon the left and fairest part of my otterskin waistcoat.

Old Sir Ensor looked much astonished. For forty years he had been obeyed and feared by all around him; and he knew that I had feared him vastly, before I got hold of Lorna. And indeed, I was still afraid of him; only for loving Lorna so, and having to protect her.

Then I made him a bow, to the very best of all I had learned both at Tiverton and in London; after that I waited for him to begin, as became his age and rank in life.

" Ye two fools ! " he said at last, with a depth of contempt which no words may utter: " ye two fools ! "

" May it please your worship," I answered softly; " may be we are not such fools as we look. But though we be, we are well content, so long as we may be two fools together."

" Why, John," said the old man, with a spark as of smiling in his eyes; " thou art not altogether the clumsy yokel and the clód I took thee for."

" Oh, no, grandfather; oh, dear grandfather," cried Lorna with such zeal and flashing that her hands went forward; " nobody knows what John Ridd is, because he is so modest. I mean, nobody except me, dear." And here she turned to me again, and rose upon tiptoe, and kissed me.

" I have seen a little of the world," said the old man, while I was half ashamed, although so proud of Lorna, " but this is beyond all I have seen, and nearly all I have heard of. It is more fit for southern climates than for the fogs of Exmoor."

" It is fit for all the world, your worship; with your honour's good leave and will," I answered in humility, still being ashamed of it; " when it happens so to people, there is nothing that can stop it, sir."

" Fools you are; be fools for ever," said Sir Ensor Doone at last; " it is the best thing I can wish you; boy and girl, be boy and girl until you have grandchildren."

Partly in bitterness he spoke, and partly in pure weariness, and then he turned so as not to see us; and his white hair fell, like a shroud, around him. I longed to see and know a great deal more about him.

Hence it came to pass that I, after easing my mother's fears and seeing a little to business, returned (as if drawn by a polar needle) to the death-bed of Sir Ensor. He for his part never asked for anyone to come near him. But the chief of the women said that he liked to have me at one side of his bed, and Lorna upon the other. An hour or two ere the old man died, when only we two were with him, he looked at us both very dimly and softly, as if he wished to do something for us, but had left it now too late.

" He wants something out of the bed, dear,". Lorna whispered to me; " see what it is upon your side, there."

I sought among the pilings; and there I felt something hard and sharp, and drew it forth and gave it to him. He could not take it in his hand, but let it hang, as daisies do; only making Lorna see that he meant her to have it.

" Why, it is my glass necklace! ". Lorna cried, in surprise; " my necklace he always promised me, and from which you have got the ring, John. But grandfather kept it because the children wanted to pull it from my neck. May I have it now, dear grandfather ? Not unless you wish, dear."

Darling Lorna wept again, because the old man could not tell her, except by one feeble nod, that she was doing what he wished. Then she gave me to the trinket, for the sake of safety; and I stowed it in my breast. He seemed to me to follow this and be well content with it.

Before Sir Ensor Doone was buried, the greatest frost of the century had set in, with its iron hand and step of stone, on everything.

The strong men broke three good pickaxes, ere they got through the hard brown sod where old Sir Ensor was to lie, upon his back, awaiting the darkness of the Judgement-Day. It was in the little chapel yard; I will not tell the name of it, because we are now such Protestants, that I might do it an evil turn; only it was the little place where Lorna's Aunt Sabina lay.

I heard from Gwenny afterwards that both Carver and the Counsellor had vowed a fearful vengeance on me. They had not dared to meddle with me while the chief lay dying; nor was it in their policy for a short time after that to endanger their succession by an open breach with Lorna, whose tender age and beauty held so many of the youths in thrall.

16

THE GREAT WINTER

In the very night which followed old Sir Ensor's funeral, such a storm of snow began as never have I heard or read of, neither could have dreamed it. We all went to bed soon after supper, being cold and not inclined to talk. At that time the wind was moaning sadly, and the sky dark as a wood, and the cows huddling into the great cowhouse with their chins upon one another.

In the bitter morning I arose. An odd white light was on the rafters, such as I never had seen before. I went to the window at once, of course; and at first I could not understand what was doing outside of it. It faced due East (as I may have said) with the walnut tree partly sheltering it; and generally I could see the yard, and the wood-rick, and even the church beyond.

But now half the lattice was quite blocked up, as if plastered with grey lime; and little fringes, like ferns, came through, where the joining of the lead was.

With some trouble and great care, lest the ancient frame should yield, I spread the lattice open; and saw at once that all the earth was flat with snow, and all the air was thick with snow; more than this no man could see, for all the world was snowing.

It must have snowed most wonderfully to have made that depth of covering in about eight hours. For one of Master Stickles' men, who had been out all the night, said that no snow began to fall until nearly midnight. And here it was, blocking up the doors, stopping the ways and the water-courses, and making it very much worse to walk than in a saw-pit newly used. However, I set out to save the sheep and we trudged along in a line; I first and the three other men after me, trying to keep my track, but finding legs and strength not up to it. Watch came too. For all this time it was snowing harder than it had ever snowed before, so far as a man might guess it; and the leaden depths of the sky came down, like a mine turned upside down upon us. Not that the flakes were so very large, for I have seen much larger flakes in a shower of March, while sowing peas; but that there was no room between them, neither any relaxing, nor any change of direction. We arrived at the lower meadow to find the flock had disappeared. Eventually Watch discovered where they were buried and we dug them out. Most had survived—and I carried the sixty and six survivors two at a time back to Plover's Barrows.

Of the sheep on the mountain, and the sheep upon the western farm, and the cattle on the upper burrows, scarcely one in ten was saved, from the pure impossibility of finding them at all. That great snow never ceased a moment for three days and nights; and then when all the earth was filled, and the topmost hedges were unseen, and the trees broke down from weight (wherever the wind had not lightened them), a brilliant sun broke forth and showed the loss of all our customs.

That night such a frost ensued as we had never dreamed of, neither read in ancient books, or histories of Frobisher. The kettle by the fire froze, and the crock upon the hearth-cheeks; many men were killed, and cattle rigid in their head-ropes. Then I heard that fearful sound, which never I had heard before, neither since have heard (except during that same winter), the sharp, yet solemn sound of trees burst open by the frost-blow.

This terrible weather kept Tom Faggus from coming near our house for weeks. But of all things the gravest was the impossibility of hearing, or having any token, of or from my loved one. Not that those three days alone of snow (tremendous as it was) could have blocked the country so; but that the sky had never ceased for more than two days at a time, for full three weeks thereafter, to pour fresh piles of fleecy mantle; neither had the wind relaxed a single day from shaking them. As a rule it snowed all day, cleared up at night and froze intensely, with the stars as bright as jewels, earth spread out in lustrous twilight, and the sound in the air sharp and crackling as artillery; then in the morning snow again, before the sun could come to help.

I believe it was on Epiphany morning, or somewhere about that period, when Lizzie ran into the kitchen to me, positively kissed me for the sake of warming her lips perhaps, or because she had something proud to say.

" You great fool, John," said my lady, as Annie and I used to call her, on account of her airs and graces; " what a pity you never read, John! "

" Much use, I should think, in reading," I answered, though pleased with her condescension; " read, I suppose, with roof coming in, and only this chimney sticking out of the snow! "

" The very time to read, John," said Lizzie, looking grander; " our worst troubles are the need, whence knowledge can deliver us. Now will you listen to what I have read about climates ten times worse than this; and where none but clever men can live ? "

" Impossible for me to listen now. I have hundreds of things to see to: but I will listen after breakfast to your foreign climates, child. Now attend to mother's hot coffee."

When I had done my morning's work, I listened to her patiently. She told me of the " Arctic Regions", as they call some places a long way north, where the Great Bear lies all across the heavens, and no sun is up, for whole months at a time. Yet people managed to get along, and make the time of the year to each other by a little cleverness. For seeing how the snow was spread lightly over everything, covering up the hills and valleys and the fore-skin of the sea, they contrived a way to crown it, and to glide like a flake along. Any man might get along with a boat on either foot to prevent his sinking.

She told me how these boats were made; very strong and very light, of ribs with skin across them; five feet long and one foot wide; and turned up at each end, even as a canoe is.

But she did not tell me, nor did I give it a moment's thought myself, how. hard it was to walk upon them without early practice. Then she told me another thing concerning the use of sledges, and the power of their gliding and the lightness of their following; all of which I could see at once through knowledge of our farm-sleds, which we employ in lieu of wheels, used in flatter districts.

Therefore I fell to at once, upon that hint from Lizzie, and being used to thatching work, and the making of traps, and so on, before very long I built myself a pair of strong and light snow-shoes, framed of ash and ribbed with withy, with half-tanned calf skin stretched across, and an inner sole to support my feet. At first I could not walk at all, but after a while I grew more expert, discovering what my errors were. And this made such a difference that I crossed the farm-yard and came back again (though turning was the worst thing of all) without so much as falling once, or getting my staff entangled. Before dark that day, I could get along pretty freely: especially improving every time, after leaving off and resting.

17

BROUGHT HOME AT LAST

When, having obtained mother's consent, I started on my road across the hills and valleys (which now were pretty much alike) the utmost I could hope to do was to gain the crest of hills, and look into the Doone Glen. Hence I might at least descry whether Lorna still was safe, by the six nests still remaining, and the view of the Captain's house. When I was come to Glen Doone, not a patch of grass was there, not a black branch of a tree; all was white; and the little river flowed beneath an arch of snow, if it managed to flow at all.

And now it struck me all at once that perhaps Lorna's ewer was frozen, and perhaps her window would not shut any more than mine would; and perhaps she wanted blankets.

I resolved to slide the cliffs, and bravely go to Lorna, as no man could catch me in my snow-shoes, guns would not go off and no-one was about. It helped me much in this resolve, that the snow came on again.

Lorna's house was partly drifted up, though not so much as ours was; and I crossed the little stream almost without knowing that it was under me. At first, being pretty safe against interference from the other huts, by virtue of the blinding snow and the difficulty of walking, I examined all the windows; but these were coated so with ice that no one could so much as guess what might be inside them.

Taking nothing by this movement, I ventured to the door and knocked. I heard a pattering of feet and a whispering going on, and then a shrill voice through the keyhole, asking, " Who's there ? "

"Only me, John Ridd," I answered; and then the door was opened about a couple of inches, with a bar behind it still; and then the little voice went on:

" Put thy finger on, young man, with the old ring on it. But mind thee, if it be the wrong one, thou shalt never draw it back gain."

Laughing at Gwenny's mighty threat, I showed my finger in the opening: upon which she let me in, and barred the door again like lightning.

" What is the meaning of all this, Gwenny ? " I asked, as I slipped about on the floor, for I could not stand there firmly with my great snow-shoes on.

" Maning enough, and bad maning too," the Cornish girl made answer. " Us be shut in here, and starving, and durstn't let anybody in upon us. I wish thou wer't good to ate, young man; I could manage most of thee."

I meanwhile was wondering much within myself why Lorna did not come to me. But presently I knew the cause; for Gwenny called me and I ran, and found my darling quite unable so much as to speak. She had fainted away.

Hearing that I had some more bread, the starving girl could resist the crust of rye bread no longer, but tore it in two and swallowed half, before I had coaxed my Lorna back to sense, and hope, and joy, and love.

"I never expected to see you again. I had made up my mind to die, John; and to die without you knowing it."

"Eat up your bit of brown bread, Gwenny. It is not good enough for your mistress. Bless her heart, I have something here such as she never tasted the like of, being in such appetite. Look here, Lorna; smell it first. I have had it ever since Twelfth-day, and kept it all the time for you. Annie made it. That is enough to warrant it good cooking."

And then I showed my great mince-pie in a bag of tissue paper and gave it to them. Lorna had as much as she could do to finish her own half of pie; whereas Gwenny Carfax (though generous more than greedy) ate up hers without winking, after finishing the brown loaf; and then I begged to know the meaning of this state of things.

"The meaning is sad enough," said Lorna; "and I see no way out of it. We are both to be starved until I let them do what they like with me."

"That is to say, until you choose to marry Carver Doone, and be slowly killed by him."

"Slowly! No, John, quickly. I hate him with such bitterness, that less than a week would kill me."

"Not a doubt of that," said Gwenny: "oh, she hates him nicely then: but not half so much as I do."

Then I spoke with a strange tingle upon both sides of my heart:

"If I warrant to take you safe, and without much fright or hardship, Lorna, will you come with me?"

"To be sure I will, dear," said my beauty with a smile and a glance to follow it; "I have small alternative, to starve or go with you, John."

"Gwenny, have you courage for it? Will you come with your young mistress?"

"Will I stay behind?" cried Gwenny, in a voice that settled it. And so we began to arrange about it; it could not be too quickly done.

" Come to this frozen window, John, and see them light the stack-fire. They will little know who looks at them. The Doones are firing Dunkery Beacon, to celebrate their new captain."

" But how could they bring it here through the snow? If they have sledges, I can do nothing."

" They brought it before the snow began."

In this I saw great obstacle to what I wished to manage. For when this pyramid should be kindled thoroughly, and pouring light and blazes round, would not the valley be like a white room full of candles? But what an opportunity! All the Doones would be drunk, of course, in about three hours' time, and as for the fire, it must sink in about three hours or more, and only cast uncertain shadows friendly to my purpose.

So I told her in a few short words how I hoped to manage the escape: " Sweetest, in two hours' time, I shall be again with you. Keep the bar up and have Gwenny ready to answer anyone. Have everything you care to take in a very little compass; and Gwenny must have no baggage. I shall knock loud, and then wait a little; then knock twice, very softly."

I hastened home at my utmost speed, and told my mother for God's sake to keep the house up until my return, and to have plenty of fire blazing and plenty of water boiling, and food enough hot for a dozen people, and the best bed aired with the warming-pan. Dear mother smiled softly at my excitement, though her own was not much less, I am sure, and enhanced by sore anxiety. Then I gave very strict directions to Annie, and praised her a little and kissed her; and I even endeavoured to flatter Eliza, lest she should be disagreeable.

After this, I took some brandy, both within and about me; the former because I had sharp work to do; and the latter in fear of whatever might happen, in such great cold, to my comrades. Also I carried some other provisions, grieving much at their coldness; and then I went to the upper linhay, and took our new light ponysledd, which ran as sweetly as if it had been made for the snow

I girded my own body with a dozen turns of hay-rope, and put a good piece of spare rope in the sledd, and the cross-seat with the back to it, which was stuffed with our own wool, as well as two or three fur coats: then just as I was starting, out came Annie with a lanthorn in one hand.

"Oh, John, here is the most wonderful thing! Mother has never shown it before—a most magnificent sealskin cloak, worth fifty pounds, or a farthing."

Bidding Annie to thank mother, I drew my traces hard, and set my ashen staff into the snow, and struck out with my best foot foremost (the best one at snow shoes, I mean) and the sledd came after me as lightly as a dog might follow; and Annie with the lanthorn seemed to be left behind and waiting, like a pretty lamp-post.

The full moon rose as bright behind me as a patin of pure silver. I quickly reached the Doone Valley and, leaving the sledd where I had first seen my Lorna, I penetrated the glen. The stack-fire was still burning strongly with children playing about it, watched by their mothers. But the men were all gathered in one or two huts.

I reached Lorna's house, but received no answer to my knocks, so I pushed open the door. There in Lorna's room, I saw, by the moonlight flowing in, a sight which drove me beyond sense.

Lorna was behind a chair, crouching in the corner, with her hands up, and a crucifix, or something that looked like it. In the middle of the room lay Gwenny Carfax, stupid yet with one hand clutching the ankle of a struggling man. Another man stood above my Lorna, trying to draw the chair away. In a moment I had him round the waist, and he went out of the window with a mighty crash of glass. Then I took the other man by the neck, and he could not plead for mercy. I bore him out of the house as lightly as I would bear a baby and saw that I carried Marwood de Whichehalse. I cast him from me into a snowdrift, which closed over him.

Then I looked for the other fellow, and found him lying stunned and bleeding. Charleworth Doone, if his gushing blood did not much mislead me.

It was no time to linger now: I fastened my shoes in a moment and caught up my own darling with her head upon my shoulder, where she whispered faintly; and telling Gwenny to follow me, or else I would come back for her if she could not walk the snow, I ran the whole distance to my sledd, caring not'who might follow me. Then by the time I had set up Lorna, beautiful and smiling, with the sealskin cloak all over her, sturdy Gwenny came along, having trudged in the track of my snow-shoes, although with two bags on her back. I set her in beside her mistress, to support her and keep her warm; and then I hung behind the sledd and launched it down the steep and dangerous way.

Lorna was now so far oppressed with the troubles of the evening, and the joy that followed them, as well as by the piercing cold, and the difficulty of breathing, that she lay quite motionless, like fairest wax in the moonlight—when we stole a glance at her, beneath the dark folds of the cloak; and I thought that she was falling into the heavy snow-sleep, whence there is no awaking.

Therefore I drew my traces tight, and set my whole strength to the business; and we slipped along at a merry pace, although with many joltings, which must have sent my darling out into the cold snowdrifts, but for the short strong arm of Gwenny. And so in about an hour's time we reached Plover's Barrows. Gwenny jumped off and hung back so as not to intrude.

Betty was going to poke her broom right in under the sealskin cloak, where Lorna lay unconsious, but I caught up Betty's broom and flung it clean away over the corn chamber; and then I put the others by, and fetched my mother forward.

"You shall see her first," I said. " Is she not your daughter? Hold the light there, Annie."

Dear mother's hands were quick and trembling, as she

opened the shining folds; and there she saw my Lorna sleeping, with her black hair all dishevelled, and she bent and kissed her forehead, and only said: ": God bless her John!" And then she was taken to violent weeping, and I was forced to hold her.

"Us may tich of her now, I rackon," said Betty in her most jealous way: "Annie, tak her by the head, and I'll tak her by the toesen. No taime to stand here like girt gawks. Don'ee tak on zo, Missus. Ther be vainer vish in the zea—Lor, but her be a booty!"

With this they carried her into the house, all the women crowding around so that I thought I was not wanted among so many. Therefore I went and brought Gwenny in, to give her something to eat and to find out why she had been such a fool as to let the two vile fellows in. While she was eating she explained quite naturally that one drunken Doone had knocked loudly and the other softly, so they were let in, Lorna thinking the knocks to be my signal. I quite forgave her and went to see my dear.

That sight I shall not forget. For in the settle was my Lorna, propped with pillows round her, and her clear hands spread sometimes to the blazing fire-place. In her eyes no knowledge was of anything around her, neither in her neck the sense of leaning towards anything. Only both her lovely hands were entreating something, to spare her or to love her; and the lines of supplication quivered in her sad white face.

"All go away except my mother," I said very quietly, but so that I would be obeyed; and everybody knew it. Then mother came to me alone; and she said: "The frost is in her brain; I have heard of this before, John." "Mother, I will have it out," was all that I could answer her; "leave her to me altogether: only you sit there and watch." For I felt that Lorna knew me, and no other soul but me; and that if not interfered with, she would soon come home to me. Therefore, I sat gently by her, leaving nature, as it were, to her own good time and will. And presently the glance that watched me, as at distance and in doubt, began to flutter and to brighten, and to deepen into kindness, then to beam with trust and love, and then with gathering tears to falter, and in shame to turn away. But the small entreating hands found their way, as if by instinct, to my great protecting palms; and trembled there, and rested there.

For a little while we lingered thus, neither wishing to move away, neither caring to look beyond the presence of the other; both alike so full of hope and comfort, and true happiness, if only the world would let us be. And then a little sob disturbed us, and Lorna, guessing what it was, jumped up so very rashly that she almost set her frock on fire from the great ash-log; and away she ran to the old oak chair, where mother was by the clock-case pretending to be knitting, and she took the work from mother's hands, and laid them both upon her head, kneeling humbly, and looking up.

" God bless you, my fair mistress! " said mother, bending nearer, and then as Lorna's gaze prevailed, " God bless you, my sweet child! "

And so she went to mother's heart, by the very nearest road, even as she had come to mine; I mean the road of pity, smoothed by grace, and youth, and gentleness.

18

SQUIRE FAGGUS MAKES SOME LUCKY HITS

I very soon persuaded Lorna that for the present she was safe, and that she was not only welcome, but as gladdening to our eyes as the flowers of May. Mother could not do enough; and Annie almost worshipped her; and even Lizzie could not keep her bitterness towards her; especially when she found that Lorna knew as much of books as need be. As for John Fry, and Betty, and Molly, they were a perfect plague when Lorna came into the kitchen. For betwixt them there was no getting the dinner cooked with Lorna in the kitchen. And the worst of it all was that Lorna took the strangest of all fancies for this very kitchen; and it was hard to keep her out of it.

Although it was the longest winter ever known in our parts (never having ceased to freeze for a single night, and scarcely for a single day, from the middle of December till the second week in March), to me it was the very shortest, and the most delicious; and verily I do believe it was the same to Lorna. But when the Ides of March were come (of which I do remember something dim from school, and something clear from my favourite writer), lo, there were increasing signals of a change of weather.

About the tenth of March, the odd moaning sound which had lasted all through the weeks of frost ceased suddenly. Then the welcome rain began. But this brought other troubles as the Lynn and Bagworthy rivers rose to mighty rushing torrents, flooding the land beside the river with the spate of water caused by the melting snow.

It was now high time to be ready for a great and vicious attack from the Doones. Of farm-work there was little yet for even the most zealous man to begin to lay his hand to; because when the ground appeared through the crust of bubbled snow (as at last it did, though not as my Lorna had expected, at the first few drops of rain) it was all so soaked and sodden, and, as we call it, "mucksy", that to meddle with it in any way was to do more harm than good.

There was no keeping Lorna in the house. She had taken up some peculiar notion that she must earn her living by the hard work of her hands. It was quite in vain to tell her that she was expected to do nothing, and far worse than vain (for it made her cry sadly) if anyone assured her that she could do no good at all. She even began upon mother's garden, before the snow was clean gone from it, and sowed a beautiful row of peas, every one of which the mice ate.

But we grieved at this, as she was too fair and dainty for rough work. Was it safe to work in the garden when she could be watched or even shot at?

Now in spite of the floods, and the sloughs being out, and

the state of the roads most perilous, Squire Faggus came at last and there was a great ado between him and Annie. He had very good news to tell, and he told it with such force of expression as made us laugh very heartily. He had taken up his purchase from old Sir Roger Bassett of a nice bit of land to the south of the moors, and in the parish of Molland. Tom saw at once what it was fit for—the breeding of fine cattle. He had even turned the winter to some use, by rounding up and selling the hungry forest ponies. He asked when he could marry Annie and we told him that as he was now a man of property he could do so whenever she was ready.

Upon this I went in search of Lorna, to tell her of our cousin's arrival, and to ask whether she would think fit to see him, or to dine by herself that day. But Lorna had some curiosity to know what this famous man was like, and declared that she would by all means have the pleasure of dining with him. Two things caught Squire Faggus' eyes, after he had made a most gallant bow and received a most graceful courtesy. They were, first, and most worthily, Lorna's face, and secondly, the ancient necklace restored to her by Sir Ensor Doone.

Now when the young maidens were gone—for we had quite a high dinner of fashion that day, with Betty Muxworthy waiting and Gwenny Carfax at the gravy—and only mother and Tom and I remained at the white deal table, with brandy and schnapps and hot-water jugs, Squire Faggus said quite suddenly, and perhaps on purpose to take us aback, in case of our hiding anything:

" What do you know of the history of that beautiful maiden, good mother ? "

" Not half so much as my son does," mother answered, with a soft smile at me, " and when John does not choose to tell a thing, wild horses will not pull it out of him."

" That is not at all like me, mother," I replied rather sadly; " you know almost every word about Lorna, quite as well as I do."

Tom Faggus smiled, and when he had offered me some

rolled tobacco from his box and taken some himself, he told us that he was sure he had seen my Lorna's face before, many and many years ago, when she was quite a little child, but he could not remember where it was.

"Nevertheless," he finished, "in the name of goodness, don't let that helpless child go about, with a thing worth half the county on her."

"She is worth all the county herself," said I, "and all England put together, but she has nothing worth half a rick of hay upon her, except her ring."

"Tush, the ring!" Tom Faggus cried, with a contempt that moved me; "I would never have stopped a man for that. But the necklace, you great oaf, the necklace is worth all your farm put together, and your Uncle Ben's fortune to the back of it; ay, and all the town of Dulverton."

"What," I said, "that common glass thing, which she has had from childhood!"

"Glass indeed! They are the finest brilliants ever I set eyes on; and I have handled a good many."

Mother went at once to fetch Lorna, that the trinket might be examined before the day grew dark. My darling came in, with a very quick glance and smile at my cigarro (for I was having the third by this time, to keep things in amity); and I waved it towards her as much as to say, "you see that I can do it." And then mother led her up to the light for Tom to examine her necklace.

Lorna turned away and softly took the jewels from the place which so much adorned them. And as she turned away, they sparkled through the rich dark waves of hair. Then she laid the glittering circlet in my mother's hands; and Tom Faggus took it eagerly, and bore it to the window.

"Don't you go out of sight," I said; "you cannot resist such things as those, if they be what you think them."

"Jack, I shall have to trounce thee yet. I am now a man of honour and entitled to the duello. What will you take for it, Mistress Lorna? At a hazard, say now."

"I am not accustomed to sell things, sir," replied Lorna,

who did not like him much, else she would have answered sportively. " What is it worth in your opinion ? "

" Do you think it is worth five pounds, now ? "

" Oh, no! I never had so much money as that in all my life. It is very bright and very pretty; but it cannot be worth five pounds, I am sure."

" What a chance for a bargain! Oh, if it were not for Annie, I could make my fortune."

" But, sir, I would not sell it to you, not for twenty times five pounds. My grandfather was so kind about it; and I think it belonged to my mother."

" There are twenty-five rose diamonds in it, and twenty-five large brilliants that cannot be matched in London. How say you, Mistress Lorna, to a hundred thousand pounds ? "

Lorna took the necklace very quietly from the hand of Squire Faggus, who had not half done with admiring it, and she went up to my mother with the sweetest smile I ever saw.

" Dear, kind mother, I am so glad," she said in a whisper, coaxing mother out of sight of all but me; " now you will have it, won't you, dear ? And I shall be so happy; for a thousandth part of your kindness to me no jewels in the world can match."

I cannot tell what mother said in reply to Lorna; for when I came back, behold Tom Faggus had gotten again the necklace. He said that the necklace was made in Amsterdam, two or three hundred years ago, long before London jewellers had begun to meddle with diamonds; and on the gold clasp he found some letters, done in some inverted way, the meaning of which was beyond him; also a bearing of some kind, which he believed was a mountain cat. And thereupon he declared that now he had earned another glass of schnapps, and would Mistress Lorna mix it for him ?

I was amazed at his impudence; and Annie, who thought this her business, did not look best pleased, and I hoped that Lorna would tell him at once to go and do it for himself. But instead of that she rose to do it, with a soft humility, which went direct to the heart of Tom; and he leapt up with a curse at himself, and took the hot water from her, and would not allow her to do anything but put the sugar in; and then he bowed to her grandly. I knew what Lorna was thinking of; she was thinking all the time that her necklace had been taken by the Doones with violence upon some great robbery; and that Squire Faggus knew it, though he would not show his knowledge, and that this was perhaps the reason why mother had refused it. So Lorna wore it no more and asked me to take charge of it.

19

EVERY MAN MUST DEFEND HIMSELF

Tom Faggus took his good departure, which was a kind farewell to me, on the very day I am speaking of, the day after his arrival.

Scarcely was Tom out of sight when in came Master Jeremy Stickles, splashed with mud from head to foot, and not in the best of humours, though happy to be back again.

" Curse those fellows!" he cried, with a stamp which sent the water hissing from his boot among the embers. " A pretty plight you may call this, for His Majesty's Commissioner to return to his headquarters in! Annie, my dear," for he was always very affable with Annie, " will you help me off with my overalls, and then turn your pretty hand to the gridiron ? Not a blessed morsel have I touched for more than twenty-four hours."

He told us now that three Doones had pursued him as he was coming from South Molton with a trooper with him as escort. They had shot and killed the trooper, but his own life had been saved by a little stone bottle of eau-de-vie he had slung from his waist.

Jeremy later led me aside in the course of the evening and told me the result of his journey; saying that I knew as well as he did, that it was not women's business. This I took, as it was meant, for a gentle caution that Lorna (whom he had not seen as yet) must not be informed of any of his doings.

Master Stickles complained that the weather had been against him bitterly, closing all the roads around him, even as it had done with us. It had taken him eight days, he said, to get from Exeter to Plymouth; whither he found that most of the troops had been drafted off from Exeter with orders not to leave the coast. The local train-bands of Devon and Somerset at first refused to fight in the other's county—the Doone Valley being on the border—but Jeremy was able to get a promise of two hundred foot when the roads were better, and not before. And meanwhile, what were we to do, abandoned as we were to the mercies of the Doones, with only our own hands to help us?

I went down to Lynmouth after consultation with Jeremy, taking the higher roads to avoid the floods. I returned with Will Watcombe and three other men, one of whom was Stickles' chief mate. On the return journey we added two more to our company—the watchmen from the Foreland.

It was lucky that I came home so soon; for I found the house in great commotion, and all the women trembling. When I asked what the matter was, Lorna, who seemed the most self-possessed, answered that it was all her fault, for she alone had frightened them. And this in the following manner. She had stolen out to the garden towards dusk, to watch some favourite hyacinths just pushing up, like a baby's teeth, and just attracting the fatal notice of a great house-snail at night-time. Lorna at last had discovered the glutton, and was bearing him off in triumph to the tribunal of the ducks, when she descried an oval face glaring at her stead-fastly from the elder bush beyond the stream and she knew it was the face of Carver Doone.

With his deadly smile, gloating upon her horror, he had lifted his long gun, and pointed full at Lorna's heart, then lowered it, inch by inch. When it pointed to the ground, between her delicate arched insteps, he pulled the trigger, and the bullet flung the mould all over her.

"I have spared you this time," he said in his deep, calm voice, "only because it suits my plans; and I never yield to temper. But unless you come back tomorrow, with all you took away, and teach me to destroy that fool who has destroyed himself for you, your death is here, where it has long been waiting."

Although his gun was empty, he struck the breech of it with his finger; and then he turned away, not deigning even once to look back again; and Lorna saw his giant figure striding across the meadow-land.

Now, expecting a sharp attack that night—which Jeremy Stickles the more expected, after the words of Carver, which seemed to be meant to mislead us—we prepared a great quantity of knuckles of pork, and a ham in full cut, and a fillet of hung mutton.

Before the maidens went to bed, Lorna had gone up to my mother, and thrown herself into her arms, and begged to be allowed to return to Glen Doone.

"My child, are you unhappy here?" mother asked her very gently, for she had begun to regard her now as a daughter of her own.

"Oh, no! Too happy, by far too happy, Mrs. Ridd. I never knew rest or peace before, or met with real kindness. But I cannot be so ungrateful; I cannot be so wicked, as to bring you all into deadly peril, for my sake alone. Let me go; you must not pay this great price for my happiness."

"Dear child, we are paying no price at all," replied my mother, embracing her; "we are not threatened for your sake only. Ask John, he will tell you. He knows every bit about politics, and this is a political matter."

She came to me, and her eyes alone asked a hundred questions, which I rather had answered upon her lips, than troubled her pretty ears with them.

"Shall I tell you what I think, John? It is only a fancy of mine, and perhaps it is not worth telling."

"Let us have it, dear, by all means. You know so much about their ways."

"What I believe is this, John. You know how high the rivers are, higher than ever they were before, and twice as high, you have told me. I believe that Glen Doone is flooded, and all the houses under water."

"You little witch," I answered; "what a fool I must be, not to think of it! Of course it is; it must be."

"But I am so sorry to think of all the poor women flooded out of their houses, and sheltering in the snowdrifts," said Lorna.

"You are right," I replied; "how clever you are! And that is why there were only three to cut off Master Stickles. And now we shall beat them, I make no doubt, even if they come at all. And I defy them to fire the house: the thatch is too wet for burning."

We sent all the women to bed quite early, except Gwenny Carfax and our old Betty. These two we allowed to stay up, because they might be useful to us, if they could keep from quarrelling.

I was not content to abide within the house, or go the rounds with the troopers; but betook myself to the rick-yard, knowing that the Doones were likely to begin their onset there. For they had a pleasant custom, when they visited farmhouses, of lighting themselves towards picking up anything they wanted, or stabbing the inhabitants, by first creating a blaze in the rick-yard.

Now I had not been so very long waiting in our mow-yard, with my best gun ready, and a big club by me, before a heaviness of sleep began to creep upon me.

I was awakened by Lorna. Leaping up, I seized my club, and prepared to knock down somebody.

"Who's that?" I cried. "Stand back, I say, and let me have fair chance at you."

"Are you going to knock me down, John dear?" replied the voice I loved so well; "I am sure I should never get up again, after one blow from you, John."

"My darling, is it you?" I cried; "and breaking all your orders? Come back into the house at once; and nothing on your head, dear!"

" How could I sleep, while at any moment you might be killed beneath my window? And now is the time of real danger; for men can see to travel."

I saw at once the truth of this. The moon was high, and clearly lighting all the watered valleys. To sleep any longer might be death, not only to myself, but all.

" The man on guard at the back of the house is fast asleep," she continued; " Gwenny, who let me out, and came with me, has heard him snoring for two hours. I think the women ought to be the watch, because they have had no travelling. Where do you suppose little Gwenny is?"

" Surely not gone to Glen Doone?"

" No." said Lorna, " she is perched in yonder tree, which commands the Barrow valley. She says that they are almost sure to cross the streamlet there; and now it is so wide and large, that she can trace it in the moonlight, half a mile beyond her. If they cross she is sure to see them, and in good time to let us know."

I shouldered arms and resolved to tramp till morning. For I was vexed at my own neglect, and that Lorna should have to right it. But before I had long been on duty, making the round of the ricks and stables, and hailing Gwenny now and then from the bottom of her tree, a short wide figure stole towards me, in and out of the shadows, and I saw that it was no other than the little maid herself, and that she bore some tidings.

" Ten on 'em crossed the watter down yonner," said Gwenny, putting her hand to her mouth, and seeming to regard it as good news rather than anything else; " be arl craping up by the hedgerow now. I could shutt dree on 'em from the bar of the gate, if so be I had your goon, young man."

" There is no time to lose, Gwenny. Run to the house, and fetch Master Stickles and all the men; while I stay here and watch the rick-yard."

Therefore I stood in a nick of the clover, whence we had cut some trusses, with my club in my hand and my gun close by.

The robbers rode into our yard as coolly as if they had been invited, having lifted the gate from the hinges first, on account of its being fastened. Then they actually opened our stable doors, and turned our honest horses out, and put their own rogues in the place of them. By this time I could see our troopers, waiting in the shadow of the house. But Jeremy Stickles very wisely kept them in readiness, until the enemy should advance upon them.

" Two of you lazy fellows go," it was the deep voice of Carver Doone, " and make us a light to cut their throats by. Only one thing, once again. If any man touches Lorna, I will stab him where he stands. She belongs to me. There are two other young damsels here, whom you may take if you please. And the mother, I hear, is still comely. Now for our rights. We have borne too long the insolence of these yokels. Kill every man and every child and burn the cursed place down."

I aimed at Carver but could not shoot, as I had never taken life. Therefore I dropped my carbine, and grasped again my club, which seemed a more straighforward implement.

Presently two young men came towards me, bearing brands of resined hemp, kindled from Carver's lamp. The foremost of them set his torch to the rick within a yard of me, the smoke concealing me from him. I struck him with a back-handed blow on the elbow, as he bent it; and I heard the bone of his arm break, as clearly as ever I heard a twig snap. With a roar of pain he fell on the ground, and his torch dropped there, and singed him. The other man stood amazed at this, not having yet gained sight of me; till I caught his firebrand from his hand, and thrust it into his countenance. With that he leapt at me; but I caught him, in a manner learned from early wrestling, and snapped his collar-bone as I laid him upon the top of his comrade.

While I was hesitating thus (for I always continue to hesitate except in actual conflict) a blaze of fire lit up the house and brown smoke hung around it. Six of our men had let go at the Doones, by Jeremy Stickles' order, as the villians came swaggering down in the moonlight, ready for murder. Two of them fell and the rest hung back, to think at their leisure what this was. They were not used to this sort of thing: it was neither just nor courteous.

Being unable any longer to contain myself, as I thought of Lorna's excitement at all this noise of firing, I came across the yard, expecting whether they would shoot at me. However, no one shot at me; and I went up to Carver Doone, whom I knew by his size in the moonlight, and I took him by the beard and said: " Do you call yourself a man ? "

For a moment he was so astonished that he could not answer.

" Now Carver Doone, take warning," I said to him very soberly, " you have shown yourself a fool by your contempt of me. I may not be your match in craft, but I am in manhood. You are a despicable villain. Lie low in your native muck."

And with that I laid him flat upon his back, in our strawyard, by a trick of the inner heel, which he could not have resisted (though his strength had been twice as great as mine), unless he were a wrestler. Seeing him down, they ran off in confusion, among the last being Captain Carver himself.

We gained six very good horses by this attempted rapine, as well as two young prisoners, whom I had smitten by the clover-rick. And two dead Doones were left behind, whom we buried in the churchyard without any service over them.

I was inclined to pursue the enemy, and try to capture more of them; but Jeremy Stickles would not allow it, for he said that all the advantage would be upon their side, if we went hurrying after them, with only the moon to guide us. And one thing was quite certain, that the Doones had never before received so rude a shock, and so violent a blow to their supremacy, since first they had built up their power, and become the Lords of Exmoor.

Without waiting for any warrant, only saying something

about "*captus in flagrante delicto*"—if that be the way to spell it—Stickles sent our prisoners off, bound and looking miserable, to the jail at Taunton.   Both those poor fellows were executed, soon after the next assizes.

20

TWO VISITS

Now the business I had most at heart (as everyone knows by this time) was to marry Lorna as soon as might be, if she had no objection, and then to work the farm so well as to nourish all our family. And herein I saw no difficulty; for Annie would soon be off our hands, and somebody might come along and take a fancy to little Lizzie (who was growing up very nicely now, though not so fine as Annie); moreover we were almost sure to have great store of hay and corn after so much snow.

However, my dear mother would have it that Lorna was too young, as yet, to think of being married. And another difficulty was, that as we had all been Protestants from the time of Queen Elizabeth, the maiden must be converted first. Now Lorna had not the smallest idea of ever being converted. She said that she loved me truly, but wanted not to convert me; and if I loved her equally, why should I wish to convert her ?

Lorna did, however, come to our little church, when Parson Bowden reappeared after the snow was over; and she said that all was very nice, and very like what she had seen in the time of her Aunt Sabina, when they went far away to the little chapel with a shilling in their gloves.

Everybody in our parish, ay and half the folk from Countisbury, Brendon and even Lynmouth, were to be found that Sunday in our little church of Oare. People who could not come anigh us when the Doones were threatening with carbine and firebrand, flocked in their very best clothes to see a lady Doone go to church. Now all this came of that vile John

Fry; his tongue was worse than the clacker of a charity school-bell.

Soon after this, I went over to see little Ruth Huckaback at Dulverton to make things straight with her. She received me with joy, telling me her grandfather was often away and left the business entirely to the foreman and her. Cousin Ruth told me he went off for these long visits in the shabbiest clothes and when home had no pleasure in anything except staring at bits of brown stone which he pulled out of his pocket. He certainly had something on his mind. To me Ruth was playful and coquettish, so I told her the whole story of my meetings with Lorna and my intentions of marrying her. The little thing was very quiet for a while; but then kissed me, wishing me happiness in my new life. Mother had invited her to Plover's Barrows, and although at first she wanted to come, after I had told her about Lorna, she said she could not think of visiting us.

Now while I was riding home that evening, without having seen Uncle Ben, with a tender conscience about Ruth, I guessed but little that all my thoughts were needed much for my own affairs. As I came in soon after dark, my sister Eliza met me at the corner of the cheese room, and she said: " Don't go in there, John," pointing to mother's room, " until I have had a talk with you. Do you know a man of about Gwenny's shape, nearly as broad as he is long, but about six times the size of Gwenny, and with a length of snow-white hair, and a thickness also, as the copses were last winter. He never can comb it, that is quite certain, with any comb yet invented. Lorna knows that this great man is here and knows that he wants to see her; but she begged to defer the interview until dear John's return."

I was almost sure that the man who was come must be the Counsellor himself, of whom I felt much keener fear than of his son Carver. And knowing that his visit boded ill to me and Lorna, I went and sought my dear; and led her with a heavy heart, from the maiden's room to mother's, to meet our dreadful visitor.

Mother was standing by the door, making courtesies now and then, and listening to a long harangue upon the rights of state and land, which the Counsellor was encouraged to deliver.

Then I ventured to show myself in the flesh before him, although he feigned not to see me, but he advanced with zeal to Lorna, holding out both hands at once.

"My darling child, my dearest niece, how wonderfully well you look! Mistress Ridd, I give you credit. This is the country of good things. I never would have believed our Queen could have looked so royal. Dearest Lorna, kiss your uncle; it is quite a privilege."

"Perhaps it is to you, sir," said Lorna, who could never quite check her sense of oddity; "but I fear that you have smoked tobacco, which spoils reciprocity."

"You are right, my child. How keen your scent is. It is always so with us. Your grandfather was noted for his olfactory powers. Ah, a great loss, dear Mrs. Ridd, a terrible loss to this neighbourhood. I may now be regarded, I think, as this young lady's legal guardian; although I have not had the honour of being formally appointed such. Her father was the eldest son of Sir Ensor Doone; and I happened to be the second son; and as young maidens cannot be baronets, I suppose I am ' Sir Counsellor '. As Lorna's guardian I give my full and ready consent to her marriage with your son, madam, despite an impediment—your father slew dear John's father, and dear John's father slew yours.

"Lorna Doone, stand forth from the contact with that heir of parricide; and state in your own voice, whether you regard this slaughter as a pleasant trifle."

"You know, without any words of mine," she answered very softly, yet not withdrawing from my hand, "that although I have been seasoned well to every kind of outrage, I do not believe that a word of it is true. And even if it were proved to me, all I can say is this, if my John will have me, I am his for ever."

This long speech was too much for her; she had overrated

her strength about it, and the sustenance of irony. So at last she fell into my arms, which had long been waiting for her; and there she lay with no other sound, except a gurgling in her throat.

" My sweet love, my darling child," our mother went on to Lorna, in a way I shall never forget, though I live to be a hundred; " pretty pet, not a word of it is true, upon that old liar's oath; and if every word were true, poor chick, you should have your John all the more for it. You and John were made by God, and meant for one another, whatever falls between you. Little lamb, look up and speak; here is your own John and I; and the devil take the Counsellor."

I was amazed at mother's words, being so unlike her; while I loved her all the more because she forgot herself so. In another moment in ran Annie, ay and Lizzie also, knowing by some mystic sense that something was astir, belonging to the world of women, yet foreign to the eyes of men. And now the Counsellor, being well-born, although such a heartless miscreant, beckoned to me to come away; which I, being smothered with women, was only too glad to do, as soon as my own love would let go of me.

We retired into our kitchen, whereupon the Counsellor mellowed a great deal. He drank a great deal of wine and ended by telling us he had not enjoyed an evening so much for long time.

That night the reverend Counsellor, not being in such state of mind as ought to go alone, kindly took our best old bedstead, carved in panels, well enough, with the woman of Samaria. I set him up, both straight and heavy, so that he need but close both eyes and keep his mouth just open; and in the morning, he was thankful for all that he could remember.

I, for my part, scarcely knew whether he really had begun to feel good-will towards us, and to see that nothing else could be of any use to him; or whether he was merely acting so as to deceive us. And it had struck me several times, that he had made a great deal more of the spirit he had taken than the quantity would warrant. Neither did I quite understand a little story which Lorna told me, how that in the night awaking, she had heard, or seemed to hear, a sound of feeling in her room: as if there had been someone groping carefully among the things within her drawers or wardrobe-closet.

After breakfast, the Counsellor (who looked no whit the worse for schnapps, but even more grave and venerable) followed our Annie into the dairy, to see how we managed the clotted cream, of which he had eaten a basinful. And thereupon they talked a little; and Annie thought him a fine old gentleman, and a very just one; for he had nobly condemned the people who spoke against Tom Faggus. He asked if Annie had heard that cream would set three times as hard in thrice the quantity if a string of beads or polished glass were passed over it. Annie had not, so fetched Lorna's necklace to experiment. The Counsellor passed the beads over the cream saying "Crinkleum, crankum, grass and clover," and bidding Annie to tell no one, told her to hide the necklace under a pannikin and to leave the dairy for three hours.

Meanwhile the Counsellor was gone. He bade our mother adieu, with so much high-bred courtesy of the old school, that when he was gone, dear mother fell back on the chair which he had used last night, as if it would teach her the graces.

"You had better marry him, madam," said I coming in very sternly; though I knew I ought not to say it; "he can repay your adoration. He has stolen a hundred thousand pounds."

"John," cried my mother, "you are mad!" And yet she turned as pale as death; for women are so quick at turning, and she inkled what it was.

"Of course I am, mother; mad about the marvels of Sir Counsellor. He has gone off with my Lorna's necklace. Fifty farms like ours could never make it good to Lorna."

Hereupon ensued grim silence. It was not the value of the necklace—I am not so low a hound as that—nor was it even the deplorable folly shown by everyone of us; it was the thought of Lorna's sorrow for her ancient plaything; and even more, my fury at the breach of hospitality.

But Lorna came up to me softly, as a woman should always come; and she laid one hand upon my shoulder, and she only looked at me without a word. I knew by that how I must have looked like Satan; and the evil spirit left my heart when she had made me think of it.

" Darling John, did you want me to think that you cared for my money more than for me ? "

Then Lorna went up to my mother, who was still in the chair of elegance; and she took her by both hands, and said:

" Dearest mother, I shall fret so, if I see you fretting. And to fret will kill me, mother. They have always told me so."

Poor mother bent on Lorna's shoulder, without thought of attitude, and laid her cheek on Lorna's breast, and sobbed till Lizzie was jealous, and came with two pocket handkerchiefs. And perhaps the Doones would let me have her, now that her property was gone.

21

JEREMY FINDS OUT SOMETHING

That same night, Master Jeremy Stickles (of whose absence the Counsellor must have known) came back with all equipment, ready for the grand attack.

Jeremy Stickles laughed heartily about Annie's new manner of charming the cream; but he looked very grave at the loss of the jewels, so soon as he knew their value.

" My son," he exclaimed, " this is very heavy. It will go ill with all of you to make good this loss, as I fear that you will have to do. But not a word to your mother that you will have to make it good. Likely enough I am quite wrong; and God-send that I be so. But what I guessed at some time back seems more than a guess, now that you have told me of these wondrous jewels. Now will you keep as close as death every word I tell you ? "

" By the honour of a man, I will. Until you yourself release me. Only think of loving Lorna, only think of kissing her;

and then remembering that her father had destroyed the life of mine! Jeremy, I confess to you in secret, I am not ashamed to say that a woman may look over this easier than a man may."

"Because her nature is larger, my son, when she truly loves, although her mind be smaller. Now if I can ease you from this secret burden, will you bear, with strength and courage, the other which I plant on you?"

"I will do my best," said I.

"One afternoon," began Jeremy, "some time before the accursed frost came on, I was riding from Dulverton to Watchett. Not far from the latter place the road runs close to the sea under a little cliff. Night was falling and when I beheld a house tucked under the cliff, I resolved to find out if I could rest there so as to go on to Watchett on the morrow. So I struck the door of the hostelry. Someone came and peeped at me though the lattice overhead, then the bolt was drawn back, and a woman met me very courteously. A dark and foreign-looking woman, very hot of blood I doubt, but not altogether a bad one. And she waited for me to be first to speak, which an Englishwoman would not have done.

"'Can I rest here the night?' I asked, with a lift of my hat to her; for she was no provincial dame, who would stare at me for the courtesy. 'My horse is weary from the sloughs, and myself but little better: besides that, we both are famished.'

"'Yes, sir, you can rest and welcome. But food, I fear, there is but little, unless of the common order. Our fishers would have drawn the nets, but the waves were violent. However, we have—what you call it? I never can remember, it is so hard to say—the flesh of the hog salted.'

"'Bacon!' said I. 'What can be better? And half a dozen eggs with it, and a quart of fresh-drawn ale. You make me rage with hunger, madam. Is it cruelty or hospitality?'

"'Ah, good!' she replied with a merry smile, full of southern sunshine. 'You are not of the men around here: you can think and you can laugh!'

" 'And most of all, I can eat, good madam. In that way I shall astonish you; even more than by my intellect.'

" I became not inquisitive, but reasonably desirous to know by what strange hap or hazard a clever and a handsome woman, as she must have been some day, could have settled here in this lonely inn, with a boorish husband who slaved all day in turning a potter's wheel at Watchett. And what was the meaning of the emblem set above her doorway, a very unattractive cat sitting in a ruined tree ?

"I had not very long to strain my curiosity, for when she found out I held the king's commission, she told me all.

"By birth she was an Italian, from the mountains of Apulia, who had gone to Rome to seek her fortunes, after being badly treated in some love affair. Her Christian name was Benita; as for her surname, that could make no difference to anyone. Being a quick and active girl she found employment in a large hotel; and rising gradually, began to send money to her parents. And here she might have thriven well, and married well under sunny skies, and been a happy woman, but that some black day sent thither a rich and noble English family, eager to behold the Pope. It was not, however, their fervent longing for the Holy Father which had brought them to St. Peter's roof; but rather their own bad luck in making their home too hot to hold them. Some bitter feud had been among them, Benita knew not how it was; and the sister of the nobleman who had died quite lately was married to the rival claimant, whom they all detested. It was something about dividing land; Benita knew not what it was.

" And so, in a very evil hour, she accepted the service of the noble Englishman to attend to his two children, and sent her father an old shoe filled to the tongue with money, and trusted herself to fortune.

" At first all things went well. My Lord was as gay as gay could be; and never would come inside the carriage, when a decent horse could be got to ride.

" And so they travelled through Northern Italy, and throughout the south of France, making their way anyhow;

sometimes in coaches, sometimes in carts, sometimes upon mule-back, sometimes even a-foot and weary. But always as happy as could be until the day when my Lord was killed while riding ahead to catch a view of the Pyrenee hills.

" My Lady dwelled there for six months more until her third child was born; and then at the end of October, when wolves came down to the farm-lands, the little English family went home towards their England. They landed somewhere on the Devonshire coast, ten or eleven years agone, and stayed some days at Exeter; and set out thence in a hired coach, without any proper attendance, for Watchett, in the north of Somerset. For the lady owned a quiet mansion in the neighbourhood of that town, and her one desire was to find refuge there, and to meet her lord, who was sure to come (she said) when he heard of his new infant. She would never believe he had died. Therefore, with only two serving men and two maids (including Benita) the party set forth from Exeter, and lay the first night at Bampton.

" On the following morn they started bravely, with earnest hope of arriving at their journey's end by daylight, but they were delayed at Dulverton with a broken axle. However, they pressed on over Exmoor until they came to the coast road, just before Watchett, long after dusk had fallen. And there, as Benita said, they met their fate and could not fly it. The silver light from the sea flowed in and showed them a troop of horsemen, waiting under a rock hard by, and ready to dash upon them. The postilions lashed towards the sea, till the leading horses were swimming, but soon a score of fierce men were round them. Then while the carriage was heeling over, and well-nigh upset in the water, the lady exclaimed, ' I know that man! He is our ancient enemy:' and Benita (foreseeing that all their boxes would be turned inside out, or carried away) snatched the most valuable of the jewels, a magnificent necklace of diamonds, and cast it over the little girl's head, and buried it under her travelling cloak, hoping so to save it. Then a great wave, crested with foam, rolled in, and the coach was thrown on its side, and the sea rushed in at the top and the windows, upon shrieking, and clashing, and fainting away.

" When Benita recovered her senses, she found herself upon the sand, the robbers were out of sight, and one of the serving men was bathing her forehead with sea-water. Then she arose and ran to her mistress, who was sitting upright on a little rock, with her dead boy's face to her bosom, sometimes gazing upon him, and sometimes questing round for the other one.

" Although there were torches and links around, and she looked at her child by the light of them, no one dared to approach the lady, or speak, or try to help her. Only that the Italian woman stole up softly to her side, and whispered, ' It is the will of God.'

" 'So it always seems to be,' were all the words the mother answered.

" Before·the light of the morning came along the tide to Watchett my Lady had met her husband. And now she, whom all people loved, lies in Watchett little churchyard, with son and heir at her right hand, and a little babe sleeping on her bosom.

" This is a miserable tale," said Jeremy Stickles brightly. " Hand me over the schnapps, my boy. What fools we are to spoil our eyes for other people's troubles ! "

" And what was the lady's name ? " I asked; " and what became of the little girl ? And why did the woman stay there ? "

" Well," cried Jeremy Stickles, only too glad to be cheerful again, " talk of a woman after that! The Doones took every stiver out of the carriage, and Benita could never get her wages; for the whole affair is in Chancery, and they have appointed a receiver. So the poor thing was compelled to settle down on the brink of Exmoor, and married a man who turned a wheel for making the blue Watchett ware. They have three children, and there you may go and visit them."

" Now for my second question. What became of the little maid ? "

" You great oaf! " cried Jeremy Stickles: " you are rather more likely to know, I should think, than anyone else in all the kingdoms. As certain sure as I stand here, that little maid is Lorna Doone."

When Jeremy described the heavy coach, and the persons in and upon it, and the breaking down at Dulverton, as well as the time and the weather, and the season of the year, my mind replaced the pictures, first of the foreign lady's maid by the pump caressing me, and then of the coach struggling up the hill, and the beautiful dame and the fine little boy, with the white cockade in his hat; but most of all the little girl, dark-haired and very lovely. and having even in those days the rich soft look of Lorna. Then again I recalled the helpless child whom I had seen on my return from school with John Fry, head downward lying across the robber's saddle-bow.

The King's Commissioner thought it wise, for some good reason of his own, to conceal from me, for the present, the name of the poor lady supposed to be Lorna's mother, and knowing that I could easily now discover it without him, I let that question bide awhile.

Jeremy Stickles was quite decided—and of course the discovery being his, he had a right to be so—that not a word of all these things must be imparted to Lorna herself or even to my mother, or to anyone whatever.

" If we can only cheat those confounded knaves of Equity, you shall take the beauty, my son, and the elegance and the love and all that—and, my boy, I will take the money."

" But supposing that we should both be shot in this grand attack on the valley (for I mean to go with you now, heart and soul), is Lorna to remain untold of that which changes all her life ? "

" Both shot! " cried Jeremy Stickles. " Talk not like that! And those Doones are cursed good shots too. Nay, nay, the, yellows shall go in front: we attack on the Somerset side, I think. I from behind a hill will reconnoitre, as behoves a general, you shall stick behind a tree, if we can only find one big enough to hide you. You and I to be shot, John Ridd, with all this inferior food for powder anxious to be devoured ?"

But the attack went off badly. Jeremy and I attacked the valley, hoping that the men of Somerset and Devon would do likewise. But each train band mistook the other for the enemy and whilst we alone were attacking the Doones, the men of Devon and Somerset were firing at each other, the shot passing harmlessly over the Doones. The robbers counter-attacked and captured all the cannon save one. Worst of all, Jeremy had been gravely wounded by shot from one of the Doone's cannon. This was a melancholy end to our brave setting out, and everybody blamed everyone else; and several of us wanted to have the whole thing over again, as then we must have righted it.

22

JOHN AND LORNA MEET AN OLD FRIEND

Jeremy Stickles lay and tossed, and thrust up his feet in agony, and bit with his lipless mouth the clothes, and was proud to see blood upon them. He looked at us many times, as much as to say, " Fools, let me die, then I shall have some comfort;" but we nodded at him sagely, especially the women, trying to convey to him on no account to die yet. And then we talked to one another (on purpose for him to hear us), how brave he was, and not the man to knock under in a hurry, and how he should have victory yet, and how well he looked, considering.

These things cheered him, a little now, and a little more next time; and every time we went on so, he took it with less impatience. Then once, when he had been very quiet, and not even tried to frown at us, Annie leaned over and kissed his forehead, and spread the pillows and sheets, with a curve as delicate as his own white ears; and then he feebly lifted hands, and prayed to God to bless her. And after that he

came round gently; though never to the man he had been,
and never to speak loud again.

To myself, Jeremy's wound was a great misfortune, in
more ways than one. In the first place, it deferred my chance
of imparting either to my mother or to Mistress Lorna my
firm belief that the maid I loved was not sprung from the
race that had slain my father; neither could he in any way
have offended against her family. And this discovery I was
yearning more and more to declare to them.

In the next place Colonel Stickles' illness was a grievous
thing to us, in that we had no one to command the troopers.
Ten of these were still alive, and so well approved of us that
they could never fancy aught, whether for dinner or supper,
without its being forthcoming.

Be that as it may, we knew that if they once resolved to go
(as they might do at any time, with only a corporal over them),
all our house, and all our goods, ay, and our own precious
lives, would and must be at the mercy of embittered enemies.
For now the Doones, having driven back, as everyone
said, five hundred men—though not thirty had ever fought
with them—were in such feather all round the country, that
nothing was too good for them.

But yet another cause arose to prove the need of Stickles'
aid, and calamity of his illness. Two men appeared at our
gate one day, stripped to their shirts and void of horses, and
looking very sorrowful. These two very worthy fellows—
nay, more than that by their own account, being downright
martyrs—were come, for the public benefit, from the Court
of Chancery, sitting for everybody's good and boldy
redressing evil.

Now, as it fell on a very black day (for· all except the
lawyers) Chancery had heard of Lorna, and then had seen
how rich she was; and never delaying in one thing, had
opened a mouth, and swallowed her.

The Doones with a share of that dry humour which was
in them hereditary, had welcomed the two apparitors (if that
be the proper name for them), and led them kindly down the

valley, and told them then to serve their writ. And with no more manners than that, they stripped and lashed them out of the valley; only bidding them come to us if they wanted Lorna Doone: and to us they came accordingly.

We, however, comforted and cheered them so considerably that, in gratitude, they showed their writs, to which they had stuck like leeches. And these were twofold: one addressed to Mistress Lorna Doone, so called, bidding her to come to Court when called on, and the other bidding all having custody over her to let her go. And now having Jeremy's leave, which he gave with a nod when I told him all and at last made him understand it, I laid bare to my mother as well what I knew, as what I merely surmised, or guessed, concerning Lorna's parentage.

And than I said: " Now we are bound to tell Lorna, and to serve her citation upon her, which these good fellows have given us."

" Then go and do it thyself, my son," mother replied with a mournful smile, misdoubting what the end might be. So I took the slip of brown parchment, and went to seek my darling.

" Darling," I said, " are you strong enough today, to bear a tale of cruel sorrow; but which perhaps, when your tears are shed, will leave you all the happier ? "

" What can you mean ? " she answered trembling, not having been very strong of late, and now surprised at my manner. " Are you come to give me up, John ? "

" Not very likely," I replied; " neither do I hope such a thing would leave you all the happier. Come to your little plant-house, and hear my moving story. It is of your poor mother, darling. Can you bear to hear it ? "

" Yes, I can hear anything. But although I cannot see her, and have long forgotten, I could not bear to hear ill of her."

" There is no ill to hear, sweet child, except of evil done to her. Lorna, you are of an ill-starred race."

" Better that than a wicked race," she answered, with her

usual quickness, leaping at conclusion. " Tell me I am not a Doone, and I will—but I cannot love you more."

" You are not a Doone, my Lorna, for that at least I can answer; though I know not what your name is."

" And my father—your father—what I mean is. . . ."

" Your father and mine never met one another. Your father was killed by an accident in the Pyrenean mountains, and your mother by the Doones; or at least they caused her death, and carried you away from her."

All this, coming as in one breath upon the sensitive maiden, was more than she could bear all at once; as any but a fool like me must have known. And yet she pressed my hand with hers, that now I might tell her all of it.

When at last my tale was done, she turned away, and wept bitterly for the sad fate of her parents. But to my surprise, she spoke not even a word of wrath or rancour. She seemed to take it all as fate.

" Lorna, darling," I said at length, for men are more impatient in times of trial than women are, " do you not even wish to know what your proper name is ? "

" How can it matter to me, John ? " she answered with a depth of grief which made me seem a trifler. " It can never matter now, when there are none to share it."

" Poor little soul! " was all I said, in a tone of purest pity; and to my surprise she turned upon me, caught me in her arms, and loved me as she had never done before.

In spite of Lorna's lack of interest, I hoped that she might be proved of blameless family, and honourable rank and fortune; and I now decided that if Master Stickles should not mend enough to get his speech a little, and declare to us all he knew, I would set out for Watchett, riding upon horseback, and visit the little inn with the dark and foreign-looking lady.

Now instead of getting better, Colonel Stickles grew worse and worse, and the fault of this lay purely with himself and his unquiet constitution. For he roused himself up to a perfect fever, when through Lizzie's giddiness he learned the very thing which mother and Annie were hiding from him with utmost care; namely, that Serjeant Bloxham had taken upon himself to send direct to London, by the Chancery officers, a full report of what had happened, and of the illness of his chief, together with an urgent prayer for a full battalion of King's troops and a plenary commander.

This Serjeant Bloxham, being senior of the surviving soldiers, wrote this wonderful report by the aid of our stable lanthorn. Having heard that our Lizzie was a famous judge of literature (as indeed she told almost everyone) he could not contain himself, but must have her opinion on his work.

Lizzie sat on a log of wood, and listened with all her ears up, having made proviso that no one else should be there to interrupt her. And she put in a syllable here and there, and many a time she took out one and then she declared the result so good, and the style to be so elegant, so chaste, and yet so fervent, that the Serjeant broke his pipe in three, and fell in love with her on the spot.

That great dispatch was sent to London by the Chancery officers, whom we fitted up with clothes, and for three days fattened them; which in strict justice they needed much.

Jeremy lay between life and death for at least a fortnight. At last I prevailed upon him by argument, that he must get better, to save himself from being ignobly and unjustly superseded; and hereupon I reviled Serjeant Bloxham more fiercely than Jeremy's self could have done, and indeed to such a pitch that Jeremy almost forgave him, and became much milder. And after that his fever and the inflammation of his wound diminished very rapidly.

However, not knowing what might happen, I set forth one day for Watchett, taking advantage of the visit of some troopers from an outpost, who would make our house quite safe. When I knocked at the little door of the cottage, no one came for a very long time. After a while I knocked again, and a good while after that again a voice came through the key-hole:

" Who is it that wishes to enter ? "

" The boy who was at the pump," said I, " when the carriage broke down at Dulverton. The boy that lives at oh—ah; and some day you would come to seek for him."

"Oh, yes, I remember certainly. My leetle boy, with the fair white skin. I have desired to see him, oh many, yes, many times."

She was opening the door while she was saying this; then she started back in affright, that the little boy should have grown so.

"You cannot be that leetle boy. It is quite impossible. Why do you impose on me?"

"Not only am I that little boy, who made the water to flow for you, till the nebule came upon the glass; but also I am come to tell you all about your little girl."

"Come in, you very great leetle boy," she answered with her dark eyes brightened. And I went in, and looked at her. She was altered by time, as much as I was. Yet her face was comely still, and full of strong intelligence. I gazed at her and she at me: and we were sure of one another.

Madame Benita Odam—for the name of the man who turned the wheel proved to be John Odam—showed me into a little room containing two chairs and a fir-wood table, and sat down on a three-legged seat and studied me very steadfastly. She then told me (as nearly as might be) the very same story which she had told to Master Jeremy Stickles. And being a woman, with an inkling of my situation, she enlarged upon the little maid.

"Would you know her again?" I asked, being stirred by these accounts of Lorna, when she was five years old. "Would you know her as a full-grown maiden?"

"I think I should," she answered; "it is not possible to say, until one sees the person, but from the eyes of the little girl, I think that I must know her. Oh, the poor young creature! Is it to be believed that the cannibals devoured her?"

"The little maid has not been devoured," I said to Mistress Odam, "and now she is a tall young lady, and as beautiful as can be. If I sleep in your hostel tonight, after going to Watchett town, will you come with me to Oare tomorrow, and see your little maiden? "

" I would like—and yet I fear. This country is so barbarous. And I am good to eat—my goodness, there is much picking on my bones! "

At last I made her promise to come with me on the morrow; then I set off for Watchett, to see the grave of Lorna's poor mother and to hire a cart for the next day.

And here (as so often happens with men) I succeeded without any trouble or hindrance, where I had looked for both of them, namely in finding a suitable cart; whereas the other matter, in which I could have expected no difficulty, came very near to defeat me. For when I heard from Benita that Lorna's father was the Earl of Dugal—then I never thought but that everybody in Watchett town must know all about the tombstone of the Countess of Dugal.

This, however, proved otherwise. For Lord Dugal had never lived at Watchett Grange, as their place was called; neither had his name become familiar as its owner. Someone else next in line of succession had taken possession, and had hushed up the story. So the poor Countess of Dugal, almost in sight of her own grand house, was buried in an unknown grave, together with her pair of infants, without a plate, without a tombstone (worse than all) without a tear, except from the hired Italian woman. Surely my poor Lorna came of an ill-starred family.

However, having obtained from Benita Odam a very close and full description of the place where her poor mistress lay, and the marks whereby to know it, I hastened to Watchett the following morning, before the sun was up, or any people were about. And so, without interruption I was in the churchyard at sunrise.

In the farthest and darkest nook, overgrown with grass, and overhung by a weeping tree, a little bank of earth betokened the rounding off of a hapless life. There was nothing to tell of rank, or wealth, of love or even pity; nameless as a peasant, lay the last (as supposed) of a mighty race. Only some unskilful hand, probably Master Odam's under his wife's teaching, had carved a rude L., and a ruder D., upon a large pebble from the beach, and set it up as headstone.

I gathered a little grass for Lorna, and a sprig of the weeping tree, and then returned to the "Forest Cat", as Benita's lonely inn was called, so that we could set out early, for the way is long from Watchett to Oare.

As luck would have it, the first who came to meet us at the gate was Lorna. In her joy she ran straight up to the cart; and then stopped and gazed at Benita. At one glance the old nurse knew her. " Oh, the eyes, the eyes! " she cried, and was over the rail of the cart in a moment, in spite of all her substance. Lorna, on the other hand, looked at her with some doubt and wonder; but when the foreign woman said something in the Roman language, and flung new hay from the cart upon her, as if in a romp of childhood, the young maid cried, " Oh, Nita, Nita! " and fell upon her breast, and wept, and after that looked round at us.

This being so, there could be no doubts as to the power of proving Lady Lorna's birth and rights, both by evidence and token. For though we had not the necklace now— thanks to Annie's wisdom—we had the ring of heavy gold, a very ancient relic, with which my maid (in her simple way) had pledged herself to me. And Benita knew this ring as well as she knew her own fingers, having heard a long history about it; and the effigy on it of the wild cat was the bearing of the house of Lorne.

For though Lorna's father was a nobleman of high and goodly lineage, her mother was of yet more ancient and renowned descent, being the last in line direct from the great and kingly chiefs of Lorne. A wild and headstrong race they were, and must have everything their own way. Hot blood was ever among them; and so it was only natural that an offset of the race, the Doones, who held some large property in a partnership with their kinsmen, should fall out with the Earl of Lorne, the last but one of that title.

The daughter of this nobleman had married Sir Ensor Doone; but this, instead of healing matters, led to fiercer conflict. I never could quite understand all the ins and outs of it; therefore it is enough to say, that knowing Lorna to be direct in heirship to vast property, and bearing special spite against the house of which she was the last, the Doones had brought her up with full intention of lawful marriage. If they had been next in succession the child would have gone down the waterfall to save any further trouble; but there was an intercepting branch of some honest family. Only Lorna was of the stock; and Lorna they must marry.

While we were full of these things, and wondering what would happen next, or what we ought ourselves to do, another very important matter called for our attention. This was no less than Annie's marriage to the Squire Faggus. We had tried to put it off again; for neither my mother, nor myself, had any real heart for it. Our scruple was this, that we both had great misgivings as to his steadiness.

When the time for the wedding came, there was such a stir and commotion as had never been known in the parish of Oare since my father's marriage. For Annie's beauty and kindliness had made her the pride of the neighbourhood; and the presents sent her, from all around, were enough to stock a shop with.

And now my Lorna came to me and placed her little hands in mine, and she was half afraid to speak, and dropped her eyes for me to ask.

" What is it, little darling ? " I asked, as I saw her breath come fast.

" You don't think, John, you don't think, dear, that you could lend me any money ? "

" All I have got," I answered: " how much do you want, dear heart ? "

" I have been calculating; and I fear that I cannot do any good with less than ten pounds, John."

In the end I agreed to lend her twenty pounds upon condition that I should make the purchase myself, whatever

it might be. For this end, and for many others, I set off to
Dulverton, bearing more commissions, more messages, and
more questions, than a man of thrice my memory might
carry so far as the corner where the saw-pit is.

23

I FIND OUT A SECRET
BUT LORNA GOES AWAY

Uncle Reuben was not at home, but Ruth, who received
me very kindly, persuaded me to wait for him. And by the
time that I had finished all I could recollect of my orders,
even with paper to help me, the old gentleman rode into the
yard and was more surprised than pleased to see me. I was
utterly astonished at the change in his appearance since the
last time I had seen him. From a hale, and rather heavy man,
grey-haired, but plump and ruddy, he was altered to a
shrunken, wizened, trembling and almost decrepit figure.
There was none of the interest in mankind, which is needful
even for satire.

" Come inside, John Ridd," he said. " I will have a talk
with you."

I followed him into a little dark room, quite different from
Ruth Huckaback's. It was closed from the shop by an old
division of boarding, hung with tanned canvas; and the smell
was very close and faint. Here there was a ledger-desk, and
a couple of chairs and a long-legged stool.

" Come Jack," he said, " here's your health, young fellow,
and a good and obedient wife to you. Ah, we have the maid
to suit you, my lad, in this old town of Dulverton."

" Have you so, sir? But perhaps the maid might have no
desire to suit me."

" Come now, John," said Uncle Ben, laying his wrinkled
hand on my knee, when he saw that none could heed us,
" I know that you have a sneaking fondness for my grand-
child, Ruth."

"I do like Ruth, sir," I said boldly, for fear of misunderstanding, "but I do not love her."

"Very well; that makes no difference. In any case I have at last resolved to let you know my secret; and for two good reasons. The first is, that it wears me out to dwell upon it, all alone; and the second is that I can trust you to fulfil a promise. Moreover, you are my next of kin, except among the womenkind; and you are just the man I want to help me in my enterprise."

"And I will help you, sir," I answered, fearing some conspiracy, "in anything that is true and loyal, and according to the laws of the realm."

"Ha, ha!" cried the old man, laughing until his eyes ran over, and spreading out his skinny hands upon his shining breeches, "thou hast gone the same fool's track as the rest; even as spy Stickles went, and all his precious troopers. Landing of arms at Glenthorne and Lynmouth, wagons escorted across the moor, sounds of metal and booming noises! Ah, but we managed it cleverly, to cheat even those so near to us. Disaffection at Taunton, signs of insurrection at Dulverton, revolutionary tanner at Dunster! We set it all abroad, right well. And not even you to suspect our work; though we thought at one time that you watched us. Now who do you suppose is at the bottom of all this Exmoor insurgency, all this western rebellion—not that I say there is none, mind—but who is at the bottom of it? Old Uncle Reuben!" Saying this, Master Huckaback cast back his coat, and stood up, and made the most of himself.

"Well," cried I, being now quite come to the limits of my intellect, "then after all Captain Stickles was right in calling you a rebel, sir!"

"Of course he was: could so keen a man be wrong, about an old fool like me? But come and see our rebellion, John. I trust you now with everything."

"I will give you my word," I said, although liking not such pledges. However, I was now so curious, that I thought of nothing else; and scarcely could believe at all that Uncle Ben was quite right in his head.

" Come and see our rebellion, my boy; you are a made man from tonight."

" But where am I to come and see it ? Where am I to find it, sir ? "

" Meet me," he answered, yet closing his hands, and wrinkling with doubt his forehead; " come alone, of course; and meet me at the Wizard's Slough, at ten tomorrow morning."

Knowing Master Huckaback to be a man of his word, as well as one who would have others so, I was careful to be in good time the next morning, by the side of the Wizard's Slough.

Therefore I being all alone, and on foot, preferred a course of roundabout; and starting at about eight o'clock, without mentioning my business, arrived at the mouth of the deep descent, such as John Fry described it. When I came to the foot of this ravine and over against the great black slough, there was no sign of Master Huckaback, nor of any other living man, except myself, in the silence. Therefore I sat in a niche of rock, gazing at the slough.

While yet I gazed, a man on horseback appeared as suddenly as if he had risen out of the earth, on the other side of the great black slough. At first I was a little scared, my mind being in the tune for wonders; but presently the white hair, whiter from the blackness of the bog between us, showed me that it was Uncle Reuben come to look for me, that way.

Old Master Huckaback beckoned me to come to him. Without more ado he led me in and out of the marshy places, to a great round hole or shaft, bratticed up with timber. I never had seen the like before, and wondered how they could want a well, with so much water on every side. Around the mouth there were a few little heaps of stuff unused to the daylight; and I thought at once of the tales I had heard concerning mines in Cornwall, and the silver cup at Combe-Martin, sent to the Queen Elizabeth.

" Now," said Uncle Reuben, " will you come and meet the wizard, or does your courage fail you ? "

" My courage must be none," said I, " if I would not go where you go, sir."

He said no more, but signed to me to lift a heavy wooden corb, with an iron hoop across it, and sunk in a little pit of earth, a yard or so from the mouth of the shaft. I raised it and by his direction dropped it into the throat of the shaft, where it hung and shook from a great cross-beam laid at the level of the earth. A very stout thick rope was fastened to the handle of the corb, and ran across a pulley hanging from the centre of the beam, and thence out of sight in the nether places.

" I will first descend," he said; " your weight is too great for safety. When the bucket comes up again, follow me, if your heart is good."

Then he whistled down with a quick sharp noise, and a whistle from below replied: and he clomb into the vehicle, and the rope ran through the pulley, and Uncle Ben went merrily down, and was out of sight before I had time to think of him. Up came the bucket again, and with a short, sad prayer, I went into whatever might happen.

The scoopings of the sides grew black, and the patch of sky above more blue, as, with many thoughts of Lorna, a long way underground I sank. Then I was fetched up at the bottom. Two great torches of bale-resin showed me all the darkness, one being held by Uncle Ben and the other by a short square man with a face which seemed well-known to me.

" Hail to the world of gold, John Ridd!" said Master Huckaback, smiling in the old dry manner. " Bigger coward never came down the shaft, now did he, Carfax ? "

" They be all alike," said the short square man; " fust time as they does it."

For my part, I had naught to do but look about me. For here was a little channel grooved with posts on either side of it, and ending with a heap of darkness, whence the sight came back again; and there was a scooped place like a funnel, but pouring only to darkness.

" You seem to be disappointed, John," said Uncle Reuben, looking blue by the light of the flambeaux. " Did you expect to see the roof of gold, and the sides of gold, and the floor of gold, John Ridd ? "

" Ha, ha! " cried Master Carfax. " I reckon her did; no doubt her did."

" You are wrong," I replied, " but I did expect to see something better than dirt and darkness."

" Come on then, my lad, and we shall show you something better. We want your great arm on here, for a job that has beaten the whole of us."

With these words Uncle Ben led the way along a narrow passage, roofed with rock, and floored with slate-coloured shale and shingle, and winding in and out until we stopped at a great stone block or boulder lying across the floor, and as big as my mother's best oaken wardrobe. Beside it were several sledge-hammers, some battered and some with broken helves.

" Thou great villian! " cried Uncle Ben, giving the boulder a little kick. " I believe thy time has come at last. Now John, give us a sample of the things they tell of thee. Take the biggest of them sledge-hammers and crack this rogue in two for us. We have tried at him for a fortnight, and he is a nut worth cracking. But we have no man who can swing that hammer, though all in the mine have handled it."

" I will do my very best," said I, pulling off my coat and waistcoat, as if I were going to wrestle; " but I fear he will prove too tough for me."

" Dost think to see the gold come tumbling out, like the kernel of a nut, thou zany ? " asked Uncle Reuben pettishly. " Now wilt thou crack it or wilt thou not ? For I believe thou canst do it, though only a lad of Somerset."

To me there appeared to be nothing at all remarkable about the boulder, except that it sparkled here and there when the flash of the flame fell on it. A great, obstinate, oblong, sullen stone; how could it be worth the breaking, except for making roads with? Then having lashed three hammers together, I swung me on high to the swing of the sledge, as a thresher bends back to the rise of his flail, and with all my power descending delivered the ponderous onset. Crashing and crushed the great stone fell over, and threads of sparkling gold appeared in the jagged sides of the breakage.

"How now, Simon Carfax?" cried Uncle Ben triumphantly. "Wilt thou find a man in Cornwall can do the like of that?"

"Ay, and more," he answered. "However, it be pretty fair for a lad of these outlandish parts. Get your rollers, my lads, and lead it to the crushing engine."

All the miners had flocked to know what might be doing and I was glad to have been of some service to them: for it seems that this great boulder had been too large to be drawn along easily, and too hard to crack. But now they moved it very easily, taking piece by piece, and carefully picking up the fragments.

"Thou hast done us a good turn, my lad," said Uncle Reuben, as the others passed out of sight at the corner; "and now I will show thee the bottom of a very wondrous mystery. But we must not do it more than once, for the time of day is the wrong one."

The whole affair being a mystery to me, and far beyond my understanding, I followed him softly without a word. He led me through small passages, to a hollow place near the descending shaft, where I saw a most extraordinary monster fitted up. In form it was like a great coffee-mill, such as I had seen in London, only a thousand times larger, and with a heavy windlass to work it.

"Put in a barrow-load of the smoulder," said Uncle Ben to Carfax; "and let them work the crank, for John to understand a thing or two."

"At this time o' day!" cried Simon Carfax; "and the watching as has been of late."

However, he did it without more remonstrance; pouring

into the scuttle at the top of the machine about a basketful of broken rock; and then a dozen men went to the wheel and forced it round, as sailors do. Upon that such a hideous noise arose as I never should have believed any creature capable of making; and I ran to the well of the mine for air, and to ease my ears if possible.

" Enough, enough! " shouted Uncle Ben, by the time I was nearly deafened. " We will digest our goodly boulder, after the devil is come abroad for his evening work. Now, John, not a word about what you have learned: but henceforth you will not be frightened by the noise we make at dusk."

I could not deny but what this was very clever management. If they could not keep the echoes of the upper air from moving, the wisest plan was to open their valves during the falling evening; when folk would rather be driven away, than drawn into the wilds and quagmires, by a sound so deep and awful coming through the darkness.

This deep digging and great labour for Exmoor gold seemed to me a dangerous and unholy enterprise. And Master Huckaback confessed that up to the present time, his two partners and himself (for they proved to be three adventurers) had put into the earth more gold than they had taken out of it. Their venture had remained a secret owing to them bringing in supplies by night, the suspicions of rebellion, and the terror of the Doones. Both these last had kept folk from being too inquisitive.

But when I told Lorna—whom I could trust in any matter of secrecy, as if she had never been a woman—all about my great descent, and the honeycombing of the earth, and the mournful noise at eventide, when the gold was under the crusher, and bewailing the mischief it must do, then Lorna's chief desire was to know more about Simon Carfax.

" It must be our Gwenny's father," she cried; " the man who disappeared underground, and whom she has ever been seeking."

Before bidding her to tell Gwenny, I returned to the mine

to find out. At the bottom Master Carfax met me, being captain of the mine, and desirous to know my business. He wore a loose sack round his shoulders, and his beard was two feet long.

" My business is to speak with you," I told him. " Did you not bring from Cornwall a little maid named ' Gwenny ' and supposed to be your daughter ? "

" Ay, and she was my daughter, my last and only child of five; and for her I could give this mine, and all the gold will ever come from it."

" You shall have her, without either mine or gold, if you only prove to me that you did not abandon her."

" Abandon her! I abandon Gwenny! " he cried with such a rage of scorn, that I at once believed him. " They told me she was dead, and crushed, and buried in the drift here; and half my heart died with her. The Almighty blast their mining work if the scoundrels lied to me! "

" The scoundrels must have lied to you," I answered, with a spirit fired by his heat of fury. " The maid is living and with us. Come up and you shall see her."

" Rig the bucket," he shouted out along the echoing gallery; and then he fell against the wall, and through the grimy sack I saw the heaving of his breast, as I have seen my opponent's chest, in a long hard bout of wrestling. For my part, I could do no more than hold my tongue, and look at him.

Without another word we rose to the level of the moors and mires; neither would Master Carfax speak, as I led him across the barrows. In this he was welcome to his own way, for I do love silence; so little harm can come of it. And though Gwenny was no beauty, her father might be fond of her.

So I put him in the cow-house (not to frighten the little maid), and went and fetched his Gwenny forth from the back kitchen, where she was fighting, as usual, with our Betty.

" Come along, you little Vick," I said, for so we called her;

" I have a message to you, Gwenny, from the Lord in Heaven."

"Don't 'ee talk about He," she answered. "Her have long forgatten me."

"That He has never done, you stupid. Come and see who is in the cow-house."

Gwenny knew; she knew in a moment. Looking into my eyes she knew; and hanging back from me to sigh, she knew it even better. She had not much elegance of emotion, being flat and square all over, but none the less for that her heart came quick, and her words came slowly.

"Oh, Jan, you are too good to cheat me. Is it a joke you are putting upon me?"

I answered her with a gaze alone; and she tucked up her clothes and followed me, because the road was dirty. Then I opened the door just wide enough for the child to go to her father; and left those two to have it out, as might be most natural. And they took a long time about it.

Meanwhile I must needs go and tell my Lorna all the matter; and her joy was almost as great as if she herself had found a father. And the wonder of the whole was this, that I got all the credit; of which not a thousandth part belonged by right and reason to me.

Not long afterwards another incident added to my credit, for, having heard of a giant who was growing up in Cornwall, I must needs challenge him to a fight. This, by good fortune, I won and hastened home to tell them all.

Now, coming into the kitchen with all my cash in my breeches pocket (golden guineas, with an elephant on them for the stamp of the guinea company), I found my dear mother most heartily glad to see me safe and sound again. But by the way they hung about I knew that something was wrong.

"Where is Lorna?" I asked at length, after trying not to ask it. "I want her to come and see my money. She never saw so much before."

"Alas!" said my mother, with a heavy sigh; "she will see

163

a great deal more, I fear; and a deal more than is good for her. Whether you ever see her again will depend upon her nature, John."

"What do you mean, mother? Have you quarrelled? Why does not Lorna come to me? Am I never to know?"

"The Lady Lorna Dugal," said Lizzie, screwing up her lips as if the title were too grand, "is gone to London, brother John; and not likely to come back again. She could not help herself and she wept enough to break ten hearts. But she left a letter for 'poor John'."

Without another word I rushed (so that every board in the house shook) up to my lost Lorna's room, and tore the little wall-niche open, and espied my treasure. Part of it ran as follows—the other parts it behoves me not to open out to strangers: "My own love, and sometime lord—Take it not amiss of me, that even without farewell, I go; for I cannot persuade the men to wait, your return being doubtful. My great uncle, some grand lord, is awaiting me at Dunster, having fear of venturing too near this Exmoor country. He is appointed my guardian and master; and I must live beneath his care, until I am twenty-one years old. To me this appears a dreadful thing, and very unjust and cruel; for why should I lose my freedom, through heritage of land and gold? I offered to abandon all if they would only let me go: I went down on my knees to them, and said I wanted titles not, neither land, nor money; only to stay where I was, where first I had known happiness. But they only laughed and called me 'child', and said I must talk of that to the King's High Chancellor. Their orders they had and must obey them; and Master Stickles was ordered too to help, as the King's Commissioner. And then, although it pierced my heart not to say one 'Goodbye, John', I was glad upon the whole that you were not here to dispute it. For I am almost certain you would not, without force to yourself, have let your Lorna go to people who never, never can care for her."

She finished with these noble lines: "Of one thing rest you well assured—and I do hope that it may prove of service to your rest, love, else would my own be broken—no difference of rank or fortune, or of life itself, shall ever make me swerve from truth to you. We have passed through many troubles, dangers and dispartments, but never yet was doubt between us; neither ever shall be. Your own Lorna Dugal."

24

SLAUGHTER IN THE MARSHES

My thoughts were black all that winter and I longed for the snow and frost of the previous one, as that winter I had Lorna. What saddened me was that no message ever came to me from her, though we heard that her beauty was the talk of London.

Meanwhile, the political situation was altered by the sudden death of King Charles the Second and the accession of King James the Second. Immediately rumours began to circulate about the Duke of Monmouth. I firmly refused to have anything to do with the rebellion, and thanks to my influence no one supported Monmouth from our parish or those in the neighbourhood. There were rumours of battles—victories of the Duke at Axminster and Bridport—others said he had been defeated. Some said he had been proclaimed King of England and that all the country from Bristol westward was welcoming him. However, I determined to stay out of this, having troubles of my own. For a while we were cheered by the news that Annie had had a baby, called " John " after me but even here there was sadness, for one day, at the beginning of July, I came home from mowing and saw a little cart with iron brakes underneath it, such as fastidious people use to deaden the jolting of the road. It was our Annie, with my godson in her arms, and looking pale and tear-begone. And at first she could not speak to me, but presently having sat down a little and received much praise for the baby, she smiled and blushed and found her tongue, as if she had never gone from us.

" John, I am in such trouble. All this talk is make-believe.

Tom has gone off with the rebels, and you must, oh, you must, go after him."

Moved as I was by Annie's tears and gentle style of coaxing, and most of all by my love for her, I yet declared that I could not go and leave our house and homestead, far less my dear mother and Lizzie, at the mercy of the merciless Doones.

Next morning I made the same objection to her second request; but to my amazement she produced a guarantee, signed by the Doones, that they would not attack Plover's Barrows. She had entered the valley by a disguise and Sir Counsellor had readily given her his written promise now that Lorna was not there and he had the diamond necklace. There were far fewer Doones there as many had joined the rebel camp.

Now look at it as I would, there was no excuse left for me after the promise given. Dear Annie had not only cheated the Doones, but also had gotten the best of me by a pledge to a thing impossible. And I bitterly said, " I am not like Lorna: a pledge once given, I keep it."

" I will not have a word against Lorna," cried Annie; " I will answer for her truth, as surely as I would for my own or yours, John." And with that she vanquished me.

Right early in the morning I was off. I took good Kickums, who (although with one eye spoiled) was worth ten sweet-tempered horses to a man who knew how to manage him; and being well charged both with bacon and powder, forth I set on my wild-goose chase.

I first visited Dulverton and called on Uncle Reuben. Only little Ruth was there. She urged me not to risk the dangers of the battlefield on my fool's errand, but I could not be dissuaded.

We rattled away at a merry pace, out of the town of Dulverton; my horse being gaily fed and myself quite fit again for going.

The manner in which I was bandied about by false information from pillar to post, or at other times driven quite out of my way by the presence of the King's soldiers, may be known by the names of the following towns, to which I was sent in succession—Bath, Frome, Wells, Wincanton, Glastonbury, Shepton, Bradford, Axbridge, Somerton and Bridgewater.

This last place I reached on a Sunday night, the fourth or fifth of July, I think—or it might be the sixth for that matter; inasmuch as I had been too much worried to get the day of the month at church. Only I know that my horse and myself were glad to come to a decent place, where meat and corn could be had for money, and being quite weary of wandering about, we hoped to rest there a little.

Of this, however, we found no chance, for the town was full of the good Duke's soldiers; if men may be called so. Having sought vainly for Tom Faggus among these poor rustic warriors, I took to my hostel and went to bed, being weary as weary can be.

Having been wakened by my landlady, who urged me to go and fight for "Zummerzett" on the rebel side, I was wide awake, though much aggrieved at feeling so, and through the open window heard the distant roll of musketry, and the beating of drums with a quick rub-a-dub, and the "come round the corner" of trumpet call. And perhaps Tom Faggus might be there and shot at any moment, and my dear Annie left a poor widow, and my godson Jack an orphan, without a tooth to help him.

I arose and dressed myself, and woke Kickums (who was snoring) and set out to see the worst of it. The sleepy hostler scratched his poll, and could not tell me which way to take; what odds to him who was King, or Pope, so long as he paid his way, and got a bit of bacon on Sunday? All this was done by lanthorn light, although the moon was high and bold; and in the Northern heaven flags and ribbons of a jostling pattern, such as we often have in autumn, but in July very rarely.

Therefore I was guided mainly by the sound of guns and trumpets, in riding out of the narrow ways and into the open marshes. And thus I might have found my road, in spite of all the spread of water and the glaze of moonshine; but that as I followed sound (far from hedge or causeway), fog (like a chestnut tree in blossom touched with moonlight) met me. At last, when I almost despaired of escaping from this tangle of spongy banks and hazy creeks and reed-fringe, my horse heard the neigh of a fellow horse, and was only too glad to answer it. Therefore, as he might know the way, and appeared to have been in the battle, we followed him very carefully; and he led us to a little hamlet, called (as I found afterwards) West Zuyland, or Zealand, so named perhaps from its situation amid this inland sea.

Here the King's troops had been quite lately, and their fires were still burning; but the men themselves had been summoned away by the night attack of the rebels. Hence I procured for my guide a young man who knew the district thoroughly, and who led me by many intricate ways to the rear of the rebel army. We came upon a broad open moor, striped with sullen water-courses, shagged with sedge and yellow iris, and in the drier part with bilberries. For by this time it was four o'clock and the summer sun, arising wanly, showed us all the ghastly scene.

Would that I had never been there! Often in the lonely hours, even now it haunts me: would, far more, that the piteous thing had never been done in England! Flying men, flung back from dreams of victory and honour, only glad to have the luck of life and limbs to fly with, mud-bedraggled, foul with slime, reeking both with sweat and blood, which they could not stop to wipe, cursing, with their pumped-out lungs, every stick that hindered them, or gory puddle that slipped the step, scarcely able to leap over the corpses that had dragged to die. And to see how the corpses lay; some as fair as death in sleep; with the smile of placid valour, and of noble manhood, hovering yet on the silent lips. And of these men there was nothing in their broad blue eyes to fear. But others were of different sort; simple fellows unused to pain, accustomed to the bill-hook, perhaps, or rasp of the knuckles in a quick-set hedge, or making some to-do, at breakfast, over a thumb cut in sharpening a scythe, and expecting their wives to make more to-do.

Seeing me riding to the front where the work of death went on, among the men of true English pluck, the fugitives called out to me, in half a dozen dialects, to make no utter fool of myself; for the great guns were come and the fight was over; all the rest was slaughter.

" Arl oop wi' Moonmo'," shouted one big fellow, a miner of the Mendip Hills, whose weapon was a pickaxe: " na oose to vaight na moor. Wend thee hame, young mon, agin."

Upon this I stopped my horse, desiring not to be shot for nothing; and eager to aid some poor sick people, who tried to lift their arms to me. In the midst of this I felt warm lips laid against my cheek quite softly, and then a little push; and behold it was a horse leaning over me! I arose in haste and there stood Winnie, Tom Faggus' mare, looking at me with beseeching eyes, enough to melt a heart of stone. Then seeing my attention fixed, she turned her head and glanced back sadly towards the place of battle, and gave a little wistful neigh; and then looked me full in the face again, as much as to say; " Do you understand? " while she scraped with one foot impatiently. If ever a horse tried to speak it was Winnie at that moment. I went to her side and patted her; but that was not what she wanted. Then I offered to leap into the empty saddle; but neither did that seem good to her; for she ran away towards the part of the field at which she had been glancing back, and then turned round and shook her mane, entreating me to follow her. I mounted my own horse again, and to Winnie's great delight professed myself at her service. With her ringing silvery neigh, such as no other horse of all I ever knew could equal, she at once proclaimed her triumph, and told her master (or meant to tell if death should not have closed his ears) that she was coming to his aid, and bringing one who might be trusted, of the higher race that kill.

A cannon-bullet fired low, and ploughing the marsh

slowly, met poor Winnie front to front. But luckily for
Winnie's life, a rise of wet ground took the ball, even under
her very nose; and there it cut a splashy groove, missing her
off hind-foot by an inch, and scattering black mud over her.

Therefore, with those reckless cannons, brazen-mouthed
and bellowing, two furlongs off, or it might be more (and the
more the merrier), I would have given that year's hay-crop
for a bit of hill, or a thicket of oaks, or almost even a badger's
earth. Nearly all were scattered now. Of the noble countrymen (armed with scythe, or pickaxe, blacksmith's hammer,
or fold-pitcher) who had stood their ground for hours against
blazing musketry, from men whom they could not get at by
reason of the water-dyke, and then against the deadly cannon,
dragged by the Bishop's horses to slaughter his own sheep;
of these sturdy Englishmen, noble in their want of sense,
scarce one out of four remained for the cowards to shoot
down. " Cross the rhaine," they shouted out, " cross the
rhaine, and coom within rache:" but the other mongrel
Britons, with a mongrel at their head, found it pleasanter to
shoot men, who could not shoot in answer, than to meet the
chance of mischief from strong arms and stronger hearts.

The last scene of this piteous play was acting, just as I rode
up. Broad daylight and upstanding sun, winnowing fog
from the eastern hills and spreading the moors with freshness;
all along the dykes they shone, glistened on the willow
trunks and touched the banks with a hoary grey. But alas!
those banks were touched more deeply with a gory red, and
strewn with fallen trunks more woeful than the wreck of
trees; while howling, cursing, yelling, and the loathsome
reek of carnage drowned the scent of new mown-hay and
the carol of the lark.

Then the cavalry of the King, with their horses at full
speed, dashed from either side upon the helpless mob of
countrymen. A few pikes feebly levelled met them; but they
shot the pikemen, drew swords, and helter-skelter leaped
into the shattered and scattering mass. Right and left they
hacked and hewed; I could hear the snapping of scythes

beneath them, and see the flash of their sweeping swords. How it must end was plain enough, even to one like myself, who had never beheld such a battle before. But Winnie led me away to the left; and as I could not help the people, neither stop the slaughter, but found the cannon bullets coming very rudely nigh me, I was only too glad to follow her.

25

JOHN GOES TO LONDON—AND LORNA

That faithful creature, whom I began to admire as if she were my own (which is no little thing for a man to say of another man's horse), stopped in front of a low black shed, such as we call a " linhay ". And here she uttered a little greeting, in a subdued and softened voice, hoping to obtain answer such as her master was wont to give in a cheery manner. Receiving no reply she entered; and I (who could scarce keep up with her, poor Kickums being weary) leaped from his back and followed. There I found her sniffing gently, but with great emotion, at the body of Tom Faggus.

Upon this I took courage and handled poor Tom, which being young I had feared at first to do. He groaned very feebly as I raised him up, and there was the wound, a great savage one (whether from pike-thrust or musket-ball), gaping and welling in his right side, from which a piece seemed to be torn away. I bound it up with some of my linen, so far as I knew how; just to stanch the flow of blood, until we could get a doctor. Then I gave him a little weak brandy and water, after which he seemed better, and a little colour came to his cheeks; and he looked at Winnie and knew her; and would have her nose in his clammy hand, though I thought it not good for either of them. With the stay of my arm he sat upright, and faintly looked about him as if at the end of a violent dream, too much for his power of mind. Then he managed to whisper, " Is Winnie hurt ? "

"As sound as a roach," I answered "Then so am I," said he. "Put me upon her back, John; she and I die together."

He told me with many breaks and pauses that unless I obeyed his orders, he would tear off all my bandages, and accept no further aid from me.

While I was yet hesitating, a storm of horse at full gallop went by, tearing, swearing, bearing away all the country before them. Only a little pollard hedge kept us from their blood-shot eyes. "Now is the time," said my cousin Tom, so far as I could make out his words. "On their heels I am safe, John, if I only have Winnie under me. Winnie and I die together." With a strong sash, I bound him upon Winnie's back.

"God bless you, John; I am safe," he whispered, fearing to open his lungs much. "Who can come near my Winnie mare? A mile of her gallop is ten years of life. Look out for yourself, John Ridd." He sucked his lips and the mare went off, as easy and swift as a swallow.

As soon as I was alone I realized how tired I was, so went to sleep in a barn until I was woken by a group of about twenty foot-soldiers. Two of them I managed to beat, and then rushed out through them and escaped on Kickums. Another company of soldiers whom I fell in with treated me well. But the first set of men joined them and a brawl took place until their officer, Colonel Kirke, rode up. He eyed me mercilessly and summarily ordered me to be shot.

A cold sweat broke out all over me, but while he was yet dwelling on the word "Fire" the hoofs of a horse dashed out on the road, and horse and horseman flung themselves betwixt me and the gun-muzzles.

"How now, Captain Stickles," cried Kirke, "dare you, sir, to come betwixt me and my lawful prisoner?"

"Nay, hearken one moment, Colonel," replied my old friend Jeremy; and his damaged voice was the sweetest sound I had heard for many a day; "for your own sake hearken."

I could not catch what passed between them but I fancied

the name of the Lord Chief Justice Jeffreys was spoken more than once, and with emphasis and deference.

" Then I leave him in your hands, Captain Stickles," said Kirke at last, so that all might hear him.

" Colonel Kirke, I will answer for him," Master Stickles replied, with a grave bow, and one hand on his breast: " John Ridd, you are my prisoner. Follow me, John Ridd."

I wrung the hand of Jeremy Stickles, for his truth and goodness; and he almost wept (for since his wound he had been a weakened man) as he answered, "Turn for turn, John. You saved my life from the Doones; and by the mercy of God I have saved you from a far worse company. Let your sister Annie know it."

Now Kickums was not like Winnie, any more than a man is like a woman; and so he had not followed my fortunes, except at his own distance. No doubt but what he felt a certain interest in me; but his interest was not devotion. Therefore seeing things to be bad, and his master involved in trouble, what did the horse do but start for the ease and comfort of Plover's Barrows, and the plentiful ration of oats abiding in his own manger. But I could not help being very uneasy at the thought of my mother's discomfort and worry, when she should spy this good horse coming home without any master.

Jeremy Stickles assured me as we took the road to Bridgewater, that the only chance for my life (if I still refused to fly) was to obtain an order forthwith for my dispatch to London, as a suspected person indeed, but not found in open rebellion, and believed to be under the patronage of the great Lord Jeffreys.

" If I fly, the farm is forfeited, and my mother and sister must starve. Moreover, I have done no harm; I have borne no weapons against the King, nor desired the success of his enemies. I like not that the son of a bonaroba should be King of England; neither do I count the Papists any worse than we are. If they have aught to try me for, I will stand my trial."

" Then to London thou must go, my son. I have influence

with Lord Churchill, and we must contrive to see him, ere the foreigner falls to work again. Lord Churchill is a man of sense and imprisons nothing but his money."

We were lucky enough to find this nobleman, who has since become so famous by his foreign victories. He received us with great civility and looked at me with much interest, being a tall and fine young man himself, but not to compare with me in size, although far better favoured. I liked his face well enough, but thought there was something false about it. He put me a few keen questions, such as a man not assured of honesty might have found hard to answer; and he stood in a very upright attitude, making the most of his figure.

I saw nothing to be proud of at the moment, in this interview; but since the great Duke of Marlborough rose to the top of glory, I have tried to remember more about him than my conscience quite backs up. How should I know that this man would be foremost in our kingdom in five-and-twenty years or so? Nevertheless, I have been so cross-questioned about His Grace the Duke of Marlborough, and what he said to me, and what I said then, and how his Grace replied to that, and whether he smiled like another man, and whether I knew from the turn of his nose that no Frenchman could stand before him; all these enquiries have worried me so, ever since the battle of Blenheim, that if tailors would only print upon waistcoats, I would give double price for a vest bearing this inscription, " No information can be given about the Duke of Marlborough."

Now this good Lord Churchill—for one might call him good, by comparison with the very bad people around him—granted, without any long hesitation, the order for my safe deliverance to the Court of King's Bench at Westminster; and Stickles, who had to report in London, was empowered to convey me, and made answerable for producing me. I did my best to send a letter to my mother through good Serjeant Bloxham, of whom I heard as quartered with Dumbarton's Regiment at Chedzuy. But that regiment was away in pursuit; and I was forced to entrust my letter to a man who said that he knew him, and accepted a shilling to see to it.

We went to London by way of Wells, Bath and Reading. The sight of London warmed my heart with various emotions, but what moved me most was the thought that here my Lorna lived and walked and took the air, and perhaps thought, now and then, of the old days in the good farmhouse. Although I would make no approach to her, any more than she had done to me, yet there must be some large chance of falling in with the maiden somehow, and learning how her mind was set. If against me, all should be over. I was not the man to sigh and cry for love, like a hot-brained Romeo: none should even guess my grief except my sister Annie.

But if Lorna loved me still—as in my heart of hearts I hoped—then would I for no one care, except her own delicious self. Rank and title, wealth and grandeur, all should go to the winds, before they scared me from my own true love.

Thinking thus, I came back to my old furrier, Master Ramsack, the which was a thoroughly hearty man, and welcomed me to my room again, with two shillings added to the rent in the joy of his heart at seeing me. By this time the Lady Lorna was high among people of fashion and was not likely to be seen out of fashionable hours.

It happened that I abode in London betwixt a month and five weeks' time ere ever I saw Lorna. From Master Ramsack I discovered that the nobleman to whose charge she had been committed, was Earl Brandir of Lochawe, her poor mother's uncle. For the Countess of Dugal was daughter, and only child, of the last Lord Doone, whose sister had married Sir Ensor Doone; while he himself had married the sister of Earl Brandir. This nobleman had a country house near the village of Kensington; and here his niece dwelled with him, when she was not in attendance on Her Majesty the Queen, who had taken a liking to her. Now since the King had begun to attend the celebration of mass in the chapel at Whitehall, he had given orders that the doors should be thrown open, so that all might see this form of worship. Master Ramsack told me that Lorna was there almost every Sunday. And the worthy furrier, having influence with the doorkeepers, kindly obtained admittance for me, one Sunday, into the antechamber.

You may suppose that my heart beat high, when the King and Queen appeared and entered, followed by the Duke of Norfolk bearing the sword of state, and by several other noblemen and people of repute. Then the doors of the chapel were thrown open and though I could only see a little, being in the corner so, I thought that it was beautiful.

Be that as it may, when the King and Queen crossed the threshold, a mighty flourish of trumpets arose, and a waving of banners. The Knights of the Garter (whoever they be) were to attend that day in state; and some went in and some stayed out. And one man I noticed was the Duke of Norfolk, who stopped outside with the sword of state, like a beadle with a rapping-rod. Then a number of ladies, beautifully dressed, being of the Queen's retinue, began to enter, but none was so well worth eye-service as my own beloved Lorna. She entered modestly and shyly, with her eyes upon the ground, knowing the rudeness of the gallants, and the large sum she was priced at. Her dress was of the purest white, very sweet and simple, without a line of ornament, for she herself adorned it. All my heart, and all my mind, gathered themselves upon her. Would she see me, or would she pass? Was there instinct in our love?

By some strange chance she saw me. Or was it through our destiny? Someone trod on the skirt of her clear white dress—with the quickness taught her by many a scene of danger, she looked up and her eyes met mine.

As I gazed upon her steadfastly, yearningly, yet with some reproach, and more of pride than humility, she made me one of the courtly bows which I do so much detest; yet even that was sweet and graceful, when my Lorna did it. But the colour of her pure clear cheeks was nearly as deep as that of my own, when she went on for the religious work. And the shining of her eyes was owing to an unpaid debt of tears.

Upon the whole I was satisfied. Lorna had seen me. Nevertheless, I waited on, as my usual manner is. A little while later, a man with a yellow beard, too thin for a good Catholic (which religion always fattens), came up to me, working sideways, in the manner of a female crab. He took my reprobate hand to save me and winked with one eye. Although the skin of my palms was thick, I felt a little suggestion there as of a gentle leaf in spring. I paid the man and he went happy.

Then I lifted up my little billet; and in that dark corner read it, with a strong rainbow of colours coming from the angled light. And in my eyes there was enough to make rainbow of strongest sun, as my anger clouded off.

Enough for men of gentle birth (who never are inquisitive) that my love told me, in her letter, just to come and see her.

I ran away and could not stop. To behold even her, at the moment, would have dashed my fancy's joy. Yet my brain was so amiss, that I must do something. Therefore to the river Thames with all speed I hurried; and keeping all my best clothes on (indued for sake of Lorna) into the quiet stream I leaped, and swam as far as London Bridge, and ate noble dinner afterwards.

26

LORNA IS STILL LORNA
BUT JOHN IS JOHN NO LONGER

When I came to Earl Brandir's house, my natural modesty forbade me to appear at the door for guests: therefore I went to the entrance for servants and retainers. Here, to my great surprise, who should come and let me in but little Gwenny Carfax. She looked ashamed, and turned away, and would hardly speak to me.

I followed her to a little room, furnished very daintily; and there she ordered me to wait in a most ungracious manner.

Almost ere I hoped—for fear and hope were so entangled, that they hindered one another—the velvet hangings of the doorway parted, with a little doubt, and Lorna, in her perfect beauty, stood before the crimson folds, and her dress was all pure white, and her cheeks were rosy pink, and her lips were scarlet. The hand she offered me I took, and raised it to my lips with fear, as a thing too good for me. "Is that all?" she whispered; and then her eyes gleamed up at me and in another instant she was weeping on my breast.

"Darling Lorna, Lady Lorna," I cried in astonishment, yet unable but to keep her closer to me, and closer; "surely, though I love you so, this is not as it should be."

"Yes, it is, John. Yes, it is   Nothing else should ever be. Oh, why have you behaved so?"

"I am behaving," I replied, "to the very best of my ability. There is no other man in the world could hold you so, without kissing you."

"Then why don't you do it, John?" asked Lorna, looking up at me with a flash of her old fun.

Now this matter proverbially is not so meet for discussion, as it is for repetition. Enough that we said nothing more than, "Oh, John, how glad I am!" and "Lorna, Lorna, Lorna!" for about five minutes. Then my darling drew back proudly; with blushing cheeks and tear-bright eyes, she began to cross-question me.

"Master John Ridd, you shall tell the truth, the whole truth, and nothing but the truth. I have been in Chancery, sir, and can detect a story. Now, why have you never, for more than a twelvemonth, taken the smallest notice of your old friend, Mistress Lorna Doone?"

"Simply for this cause," I answered, "that my old friend, and true love, took not the smallest heed of me. Nor knew I where to find her."

"Oh, you poor, dear John!" said Lorna, sighing at thought of my misery. "How wonderfully good of you, thinking of me as you must have done, not to marry that plain little thing (or perhaps I should say that lovely creature, for

I have never seen her) Mistress Ruth—I forget her name, but something like a towel."

"Ruth Huckaback is a worthy maid," I answered with some dignity; "and she alone of all our world except indeed poor Annie, has kept her confidence in you, and told me not to dread your rank, but trust your heart, Lady Lorna."

"Then Ruth is my best friend," she answered, "and is worthy of you, John. And now remember one thing, dear, if God should part us, as may be by nothing short of death; try to marry that little Ruth, when you cease to remember me. And now for the head-traitor. I have often suspected it; but she looks me in the face, and wishes—fearful things, which I cannot repeat."

With these words, she moved an implement such as I had not seen before, and which made a ringing noise at a serious distance. And before I had ceased wondering—for if such things go on we might ring the church bells, while sitting in the kitchen—little Gwenny Carfax came with a grave and sullen face.

"Gwenny", began my Lorna, in a tone of high rank and dignity, "go and fetch the letters, which I gave you at various times for dispatch to Mistress Ridd."

"How can I fetch them, when they are gone? It be no use for him to tell no lies. . . ."

"Now, Gwenny, can you look at me?" I asked very sternly; for the matter was no joke to me, after a year's unhappiness.

"I don't want to look at 'ee."

"Now, Gwenny, not to speak of that," said Lorna very demurely, "if you thought it honest to keep the letters, was it honest to keep the money?"

At this the Cornish maiden broke into a rage of honesty:

"A' putt the' money by for 'ee. "Ee shall have every farden of it." And so she flung out of the room.

"And, Gwenny," said Lorna very softly, following under the doorhangings, "if it is not honest to keep the money, it is nót honest to keep the letters, which would have been worth more than any gold to those who were so kind to you. Your father shall know the whole, Gwenny, unless you tell the truth."

" Now, a' will tell all the truth," this strange maiden answered.

Gwenny came back with a leathern bag, and tossed it upon the table. Not a word did she vouchsafe to us, but stood there, looking injured.

" Go and get your letters, John," said Lorna very gravely, " or at least your mother's letters, made of messages to you. As for Gwenny, she shall go before Lord Justice Jeffreys."

" And you may take me if you please before the great Lord Jeffreys. I have done no more than duty, though I did it crookedly, and told a heap of lies, for your sake. And pretty gratitude I gets."

" What made you treat me so, little Gwenny ? " I asked, for Lorna would not ask, lest the reply should vex me.

" Because 'ee be'est below her so. Her shanna' have a poor farmering chap, not even if her were a Carnishman. All her land, and all her birth—and who be you, I'd like to know ? "

" Gwenny, you may go," said Lorna, reddening with quiet anger; " and remember that you come not near me, for the next three days. It is the only way to punish her " she concluded to me, when the maid was gone in a storm of sobbing and weeping.

My darling and I then turned to our own problems and Lorna declared that all she wanted was to marry me as soon as she was twenty-one. She cared nothing for high life and would willingly renounce her title and fortune; though she pointed out that my education was much better than hers and that my family was as old as hers.

When I had gone, Lorna told the Earl of Brandir about our love, but he was so deaf that she never really knew if he understood. What she did not do was to tell him about the death of his son Alan Brandir, who lay beneath the sod in Doone

Valley, for his grief at this would have brought on his own death.

Meanwhile I had been able to get a letter through to mother and she had sent me a basket of food and money and presents for Lorna. There was also a letter, saying among other things that the Doones were quiet. Six had been hanged after the rebellion and this had taken the heart out of them. The farms around supplied them with their wants in return for guarantees that they would not be attacked. Tom Faggus was home and almost cured of his wound. Master Bloxham was now promoted to take the tolls and catch the rebels around our part.

And now, one day in September a piece of good fortune came my way. Having spied some rogues hanging round the Earl of Brandir's house, I engaged them in a fight which saved the Earl's life, and in which one rogue was killed and two more were captured. These I handed over to the Constable and in the morning, they were brought before the Justices of the Peace. And now my wonderful luck appeared; for the merit of having defeated and caught them would never have raised me one step in the State, or in public consideration, if they had only been common robbers, or even notorious murders. But these fellows were recognized as Protestant witnesses, the very men against whom His Majesty the King bore the bitterest rancour, but whom he had hitherto failed to catch.

In the course of that same afternoon I was sent for by His Majesty. He had summoned first the good Earl of Brandir, and received the tale from him, not without exaggeration, although my lord was a Scotsman. But the chief thing His Majesty cared to know was that, beyond all possible doubt, these were the very precious fellows from perjury turned to robbery. I was shown at once, and before I desired it, into His Majesty's presence, and there I stood most humbly and made the best bow I could think of.

As I could not advance any farther—for I saw that the Queen was present, which frightened me tenfold—His Majesty, in the most gracious manner, came down the room to encourage me. And as I remained with my head bent down, he told me to stand up and look at him.

"I have seen thee before, young man," he said; "thy form is not one to be forgotten. Where was it? Thou art most likely to know."

"May it please Your Most Gracious Majesty The King," I answered, finding my voice in a manner which surprised myself, "it was in the Royal Chapel."

Now I meant no harm whatever by this. I ought to have said the "Ante-Chapel", but I could not remember the word, and feared to keep the King looking at me.

"I am well pleased," said his Majesty, with a smile which almost made his dark and stubborn face look pleasant, "to find that our greatest subject, greatest I mean in the bodily form, is a good Catholic. Thou needst not say otherwise. The time shall be, and that right soon, when men shall be proud of the one true faith." Here he stopped, having gone rather far; but the gleam of his heavy eyes was such that I durst not contradict.

"This is that great Johann Reed," said Her Majesty, coming forward, "for whom I have so much heard from the dear, dear Lorna. Ah, she is not of this black country, she is of the breet Italie."

I have tried to write it as she said it: but it wants a better scholar to express her mode of speech.

"Now, John Ridd," said the King, "thou hast done great service to the realm and to religion. Now ask us anything in reason; thou canst carry any honours on thy club, like Hercules. What is thy chief ambition, lad?"

"Well," said I, after thinking a little and meaning to make the most of it, for so the Queen's eyes conveyed to me; "my mother always used to think that having been schooled at Tiverton, with thirty marks a year to pay, I was worthy of a coat of arms. And that is what she longs for."

"A good lad! A very good lad!" said the King, and he looked at the Queen as if almost in joke; "but what is thy condition in life?"

"I am a freeholder," I answered in my confusion, "ever since the time of King Alfred. A Ridd was with him in the Isle of Athelney, and we hold our farm by gift from him; or at least people say so. We have had three very good harvests running, and might support a coat of arms; but for myself I want it not."

"Thou shalt have a coat, my lad," said the King, smiling at his own humour, "but it must be a large one to fit thee. And more than that shalt thou have, John Ridd, being of such loyal breed and having done such service."

And while I wondered what he meant, he called to some of the people in waiting at the further end of the room, and they brought him a little sword, such as Annie might skewer a turkey with. Then he signified to me to kneel, which I did (after dusting the board, for the sake of my best breeches), and then he gave me a little tap very nicely upon my shoulder, before I knew what he was up to; and said, "Arise, Sir John Ridd!"

This astonished and amazed me to such an extent of loss of mind, that when I got up I looked about, and thought what the Snowes would think of it. And I said to the King, without forms of speech:—

"Sir, I am very much obliged. But what be I to do with it?"

27

A LONG ACCOUNT SETTLED

After this I thought it best to return to Plover's Barrows, leaving a tearful Lorna, and feeling heavy-hearted myself. To add to our troubles, as the winter passed, the Doones began to give trouble again, going so far in February as to seize Mistress Margery Badcock while her husband Christopher (a tenant farmer of Martinhoe) was away ploughing. Worse still, they brutally killed his baby son.

Now at last our gorge was risen and our hearts in tumult.

We had borne our troubles long, as a wise and wholesome chastisement; quite content to have some things of our own unmeddled with. But what could a man dare to call his own, or what right could he have to wish it, while he left his wife and children at the pleasure of any stranger?

The people came flocking all around me, at the blacksmith's forge and the Brendon ale-house; and I could scarce come out of church, but they got me among the tombstones. They all agreed that I was bound to take command and management. I bade them go to the magistrates, but they said they had been too often. Then I told them that I had no wits for ordering an armament, although I could find fault enough with the one which had not succeeded. But they would hearken to none of this. All they said was: " Try to lead us; and we will try not to run away."

Yet being pressed still harder and harder, I agreed at last to this; that if the Doones, upon fair challenge, would not endeavour to make amends, by giving up Mistress Margery, as well as the man who had slain the babe, then I would lead the expedition, and do my best to subdue them.

And then arose a difficult question—who was to take the risk of making overtures so unpleasant? I waited for the rest to offer; and as none was ready, the burden fell on me, and seemed to be of my own inviting. Hence I undertook the task, sooner than reason about it; for to give the cause of everything is worse than to have to go through with it.

It may have been three in the afternoon, when leaving my witnesses behind (for they preferred the background), I appeared with our Lizzie's white handkerchief upon a kidney-bean stick at the entrance to the robber's dwelling. Two decent Doones appeared, and hearing of my purpose, offered, without violence, to go and fetch the Captain, if I would stop where I was, and not begin to spy about anything. To this, of course, I agreed at once, because I had thorough knowledge of all ins and outs already.

Those men came back in a little while, with a sharp, short message that Captain Carver would come out and speak to me, by and by, when his pipe was finished. Accordingly I waited long. At length a heavy and haughty step sounded along the stone roof of the way; and then the great Carver Doone drew up, and looked at me rather scornfully.

"What is it you want, young man?" he asked, as if he had never seen me before.

I told him clearly to understand that a vile and inhuman wrong had been done, and such as we could not put up with; but that if he would make what amends he could by restoring the poor woman, and giving up that odious brute who had slain the harmless infant, we would take no further motion, and things should go on as usual.

"Sir John," he replied, "your new honours have turned your poor head, as might have been expected. We are not in the habit of deserting anything that belongs to us; far less our sacred relatives. The insolence of your demands well-nigh outdoes the ingratitude."

As he turned away in sorrow from me, I did my best to look calmly at him, and to say in a quiet voice: "Farewell, Carver Doone, this time; our day of reckoning is nigh."

"Thou fool, it is come," he cried, leaping aside into the niche of rock by the doorway: "Fire!"

Save for the quickness of spring, and readiness learned in many a wrestling bout, that knavish trick must have ended me: but scarce was the word "Fire!" out of his mouth, ere I was out of fire, by a single bound behind the rocky pillar of the opening. In this jump I was so brisk, at impulse of the love of life (for I saw the muzzles set upon me from the darkness of the cavern), that the men who had trained their guns upon me with good-will and daintiness, could not check their fingers crooked upon the heavy triggers; and the volley sang with a roar behind it, down the avenue of crags.

With one thing and another, and most of all the treachery of this dastard scheme, I was so amazed that I turned and ran, at the very top of my speed, away from these vile fellows: and luckily for me they had not another charge to send after me. And thus by good fortune, I escaped; but with a bitter heart and mind at their treacherous usage.

We arranged that all our men should come and fall into order with pike and musket, over against our dunghill; and we settled early in the day, that their wives might come and look at them. The wives of our band did their utmost among their relatives round about to fetch recruits for our little band. And by such means several of the yeomanry from Barnstaple and from Tiverton were added to our number; and inasmuch as these were armed with heavy swords and short carabines, their appearance was truly formidable.

Tom Faggus also joined us heartily, being now quite healed of his wound, except at times when the wind was easterly. He was made second in command to me. Also Uncle Ben came over to help us with his advice and presence, as well as with a band of stout warehousemen whom he brought from Dulverton. For he had never forgiven the old outrage put upon him; and though it had been to his interest to keep quiet during the last attack, under Commander Stickles—for the sake of his secret gold mine—yet now he was in a position to give full vent to his feelings. For he and his partners, when fully assured of the value of their diggings, had obtained from the Crown a licence to adventure in search of minerals, by payment of a heavy fine and a yearly royalty. Therefore they had now no longer any cause for secrecy, neither for dread of the outlaws; having so added to their force as to be a match for them. And although Uncle Ben was not the man to keep his miners idle one hour more than might be helped, he promised that when we had fixed the moment for an assault on the valley, a score of them should come to aid us, headed by Simon Carfax, and armed with the guns which they always kept for the protection of their gold.

Hence, what we devised was this; to delude from home a part of the robbers, and fall by surprise on the other part. We caused it to be spread abroad that a large heap of gold was now collected at the mine of the Wizard's Slough. And when this rumour must have reached them, through women who came to and fro, as some entirely faithful to them were allowed to do, we sent Simon Carfax, the father· of little Gwenny, to demand an interview of the Counsellor by night, and as it were secretly. Then he was to set forth a list of imaginary grievances against the owners of the mine; and to offer, partly through resentment, partly through the hope of gain, to betray into their hands, upon the Friday night, by far the greatest weight of gold as yet sent up for refining. He was to have one quarter part and they to take the residue. But inasmuch as the convoy across the moors, under his command, would be strong and strongly armed, the Doones must be sure to send not less than a score of men if possible. He himself, at a place agreed upon and fit for an ambuscade, would call a halt, and contrive in the darkness to pour a little water into the priming of his company's guns.

Having resolved on a night-assault (as our undisciplined men, three-fourths of whom had never been shot at, could not fairly be expected to march up to visible musket-mouths), we cared not much about drilling our forces, only to teach them to hold a musket. And we fixed upon Friday night for our venture, because the moon would be at the full; and our powder was coming from Dulverton on the Friday afternoon.

It was settled that the yeomen, having good horses under them, should help the miners near the Wizard's Slough. And as soon as we knew that this party of robbers, be it more or less, was out of hearing from the valley, we were to fall to, ostensibly at the Doone gate, which was impregnable now, but in reality upon their rear, by means of my old water-slide. For I had chosen twenty young fellows, partly miners, partly farmers and partly warehousemen, and some of other vocations, but all to be relied upon for spirit and power of climbing. And with proper tools to aid us and myself to lead the way, I felt no doubt whatever but that we could all attain the crest, where first I had met with Lorna, but, upon the whole, I rejoiced that Lorna was not present now.

The moon was lifting well above the shoulder of the

uplands, when we, the chosen band, set forth. We were not to begin our climbing until we heard a musket fired from the heights, on the left-hand side, where John Fry himself was stationed, where I had been used to sit and to watch for Lorna. And John Fry was to fire his gun, with a ball of wool inside it, so soon as he heard the hurly-burly at the Doone gate beginning; which we, by reason of water-fall, could not hear down in the meadows there.

We waited a very long time, with the moon marching up heaven steadfastly, and the white fog trembling in chords and quavers, like a silver harp of the meadows. Suddenly the most awful noise that anything short of thunder could make, came down among the rocks, and went and hung upon the corners.

" The signal, my lads," I cried, leaping up and rubbing my eyes. " Now hold on by the rope, and lay your quarter-staffs across, my lads; and keep your guns pointing to heaven, lest haply we shoot one another."

" Us shan't never shutt one anoother, wi' our goons at that mark, I reckon," said an oldish chap, but as tough as leather, and esteemed a wit for his dryness.

" You come next to me, old Ike; you be enough to dry up the waters: now remember, all lean well forward. If any man throws his weight back, down he goes; and perhaps he may never get up again; and most likely he will shoot himself."

However, thank God, though a gun went off, no one was any the worse for it, neither did the Doones notice it, in the thick of the firing in front of them. For the order to those of the sham attack, conducted by Tom Faggus, was to make the greatest possible noise without exposure to themselves until we in the rear had fallen to; which John Fry was again to give signal of.

Therefore we of the chosen band stole up the meadow quietly, keeping in the blots of shade and hollow of the water-course. And the earliest notice the Counsellor had, or anyone else, of our presence, was the blazing of the logwood house, where lived that villain Carver. It was my especial privilege to set this house on fire; upon which I had insisted, exclusively and conclusively.

We took good care, however, to burn no innocent women or children, in that most righteous destruction. For Carver had ten or a dozen wives; and perhaps that had something to do with his taking the loss of Lorna so easily. One child I noticed, as I saved him—a fair and handsome little fellow, beloved by Carver Doone as much as anything beyond himself could be. The boy climbed on my back and rode; and much as I hated his father, it was not in my heart to say, or do, a thing to vex him.

Leaving these poor injured people to behold their burning homes, we drew aside, by my directions, into the covert beneath the cliff; but not before we had laid our brands to three other houses, after calling the women forth, and bidding them go for their husbands to come and fight a hundred of us.

" All Doone-town is on fire, on fire! " we heard them shrieking as they went. " A hundred soldiers are burning it, with a dreadful great man at the head of them! "

Presently, as I expected, back came the warriors of the Doones, leaving but two or three at the gate, and burning with wrath to crush underfoot the presumptuous clowns in the valley. Just then the waxing fire leaped above the red crest of the hills, and danced on the pillars of the forest, and lapped like a tide on the stones of the slope. All the valley flowed with light, and the limpid waters reddened, and the fair young women shone and the naked children glistened.

But the finest sight of all was to see those haughty men striding down the causeway darkly, reckless of their end, but resolute to have two lives for every one. A finer dozen of young men could not have been found in the world perhaps, nor a braver, nor a viler one.

Seeing how few there were of them, I was very loth to fire, but my followers waited for no word. At a signal from old Ikey, who levelled his gun first, a dozen muskets were discharged and half the Doones dropped lifeless.

The rest of the Doones leaped at us, like so many demons. They fired wildly, not seeing us well among the hazel bushes; and then they clubbed their muskets or drew their swords, as might be, and furiously drove at us.

For a moment, although we were twice their number, we fell back before their valorous fame and the power of their onset. Yet one thing I saw, which dwelled long with me; and that was Christopher Badcock spending his life to get Charley's.

How he had found out none may tell, both being dead so long ago; but at any rate he had found out that Charley was the man who had robbed him of his wife and honour. It was Carver Doone who took her away, but Charlesworth Doone was beside him; and according to cast of dice, she fell to Charley's share. All this Kit Badcock (who was mad, according to our measures) had discovered and treasured up; and now was his revenge-time. Such a face I never saw, and never hope to see again, as when poor Kit Badcock spied Charley coming towards us.

Therefore was I not surprised, so much as all the rest of us, when, in the foremost of red light, Kit went up to Charlesworth Doone, as if to some inheritance; and took his seisin of right upon him, being himself a powerful man, and begged a word aside with him. What they said aside, I know not; all I know is that without weapon, each man killed the other. And Margery Badcock came and wept, and hung upon her dead husband; and died that summer of heart-disease.

I like not to tell of slaughter; enough that ere the daylight broke, upon that wan March morning, the only Doones still left alive were the Counsellor and Carver. And of all the dwellings of the Doones (inhabited with luxury, and luscious taste, and licentiousness) not even one was left, but all made potash in the river.

My plan to resolve the problems of who had claims on the Doone treasure was no more than this—not to pay a farthing to lord of manor, parson, or even King's Commissioner, but after making good some of the recent and proven losses—where the men could not afford to lose—to pay the residue (which might be worth some fifty thousand pounds) into the Exchequer at Westminster, and then let all the claimants file what bills they pleased in Chancery.

Now this was a very noble device; for the mere name of Chancery, and the high repute of the fees therein, and the low repute of the lawyers, and the comfortable knowledge that the woolsack itself is the golden fleece, absorbing gold for ever, if the standard be but pure; consideration of all these things staved off at once the lords of the manors, and all the little farmers, and even those whom most I feared; videlicet, the parsons. And the King's Commissioner was compelled to profess himself contented, although of all he was most aggrieved; for his pickings would have been goodly.

Moreover by this plan I made—although I never thought of that—a mighty friend, worth all the enemies whom the loss of money moved. Lord Jeffreys now being head of the law, and almost head of the kingdom, got possession of that money, and was kindly pleased with it.

And this met our second difficulty; for the law having won and laughed over the spoil, must have injured its own title by impugning our legality.

Next, with regard to the women and children, we were long in a state of perplexity. Some of the women were taken back by their parents or their husbands, or it may be their old sweethearts, and those who failed of this went forth, some upon their own account, to the New World plantations, where the fairer sex is valuable; and some to English cities; and the plainer ones to field work. And most of the children went with their mothers, or were bound apprentices; only Carver Doone's handsome child had lost his mother and stayed with me.

This boy went about with me everywhere. He told us that his name was " Ensie ", meant for " Ensor " I suppose from his father's grandfather, the old Sir Ensor Doone. And this boy appeared to be Carver's heir.

After the desperate charge of young Doones had been met by us, and broken, and just as poor Kit Badcock died in the arms of the dead Charley, I happened to descry a patch of white on the grass of the meadow, like the head of a sheep after washing-day. It was the flowing silvery hair of that sage the Counsellor. I had vowed to let him go, but was determined to get Lorna's necklace back, realizing that he alone would know where it was. I suspected it was on his person, and there indeed it was. I gave him one of the diamonds to prevent him starving and let him go. God knows what became of him.

The band of Doones, which sallied forth for the robbery of the pretended convoy, was met by Simon Carfax, according to arrangement, at the ruined house called the " Warren " in that part of Bagworthy forest where the river Exe (as yet a very small stream) runs through it.

Now Simon, having met these flowers of the flock of villainy, where the rising moonlight flowed through the weir-work of the wood, begged them to dismount, and led them with an air of mystery into the Squire's ruined hall, black with fire and green with weeds.

" Captain, I have found a thing," he said to Carver Doone himself, " which may help to pass the hour, ere the lump of gold comes by. The smugglers are a noble race, but a miner's eyes are a match for them. There lies a puncheon of rare spirit, with the Dutchman's brand upon it, hidden behind the broken hearth. Set a man to watch outside; and let us see what this be like."

With one accord they agreed to this, and Carver pledged Master Carfax, and all the Doones grew merry. But Simon, being bound as he said, to see to their strict sobriety, drew a bucket of water from the well into which they had thrown the dead owner, and begged them to mingle it with their drink; which some of them did, and some refused.

But the water from that well was poured, while they were carousing, into the priming pan of every gun of theirs, even as Simon had promised to do with the guns of the men they were come to kill. Then just as the giant Carver rose, with a glass of pure hollands in his hand, and by the light of the torch they had struck, proposed the good health of the Squire's ghost—in the broken doorway stood a press of men, with pointed muskets, covering every drunken Doone. How it fared upon that I know not, having none to tell me; for each man wrought, neither thought of telling, nor whether he might be alive to tell. The Doones rushed to their guns at once, and pointed them, and pulled them; but the Squire's well had drowned their fire: and then they knew that they were betrayed, but resolved to fight like men for it. Upon fighting I can never dwell; it breeds such savage delight in me, of which I would fain have less. Enough that all the Doones fought bravely; and like men (though bad ones) died in the hall of the man they had murdered. And with them died poor young De Whichehalse, who, in spite of his good father's prayers, had cast in his lot with the robbers. Carver Doone alone escaped, partly through his fearful strength, and his yet more fearful face; but mainly perhaps, through his perfect coolness, and his mode of taking things.

I am happy to say that no more than eight of the gallant miners were killed in that combat, or died of their wounds afterwards; and adding to these the eight we had lost in the assault on the valley (and two of them excellent warehouse-men) it cost no more than sixteen lives to be rid of nearly forty Doones, each of whom would most likely have killed three men in the course of a year or two. Yet, for Lorna's sake, I was vexed at the bold escape of Carver.

28

BLOOD UPON THE ALTAR

The thing which next vexed me was a most glorious rise to the summit of all fortune. For in good truth it was no less than the return of Lorna—my Lorna, my own darling, in wonderful health and spirits and as glad as a bird to get back again. It would have done anyone good for a twelve-month to behold her face and doings, and her beaming eyes and smile (not to mention blushes also at my salutation), when this Queen of every heart ran about our rooms again. She did love this, she must see that, and where was her old friend the cat? All the house was full of brightness, as if the sun had come over the hill, and Lorna were his looking-glass.

Lorna told us that the old Earl of Brandir had died and that the Judge Jeffreys had come to see her personally when he had heard of her fortune. The outcome of this meeting was that, in exchange for a large sum of money and royal permission, she was given her freedom to marry me. Royal permission was quickly forthcoming, so Lorna hastened back to Plover's Barrows.

Our wedding was fixed for June, and such a huge crowd wanted to attend the ceremony that the clerk decided to charge the men a shilling and the women two shillings for entering the church.

Dear mother arranged all the ins and outs of the way in which it was to be done; and Annie and Lizzie and all the Snowes, and even Ruth Huckaback (who was there after great persuasion) made such a sweeping of dresses, that I scarcely knew where to put my feet and longed for a staff to put by their gowns. Then Lorna came out of a pew half-way, in a manner which quite astonished me, and took my left hand in her right, and I prayed God that it were done with.

My darling looked so glorious that I was afraid of glancing at her, yet took in all her beauty. She was in a fright, no doubt, but nobody should see it; whereas I said, " I will go through it like a grave-digger."

Lorna's dress was of pure white, clouded with lavender (for the sake of the old Earl of Brandir), and as simple as need be, except for perfect loveliness. I was afraid to look at her, as I said before, except when each of us said " I will ", and then each dwelled upon the other.

It is impossible for any who have not loved as I have, to

conceive my joy and pride, when, after ring and all was done and the parson had blessed us, Lorna turned to look at me, with her playful glance subdued, and deepened by this solemn act.

Her eyes, which none on earth may ever equal or compare with, told me such a tale of hope, and faith, and heart's devotion, that I was almost amazed, thoroughly as I knew them. Darling eyes, the clearest eyes, the loveliest, the most loving eyes—then the sound of a shot rang through the church, and those eyes were dim with death.

Lorna fell across my knees, when I was going to kiss her, as the bridegroom is allowed to do, and encouraged, if he needs it; a flood of blood came out upon the yellow wood of the altar steps; and at my feet lay Lorna, trying to tell me some last message out of her faithful eyes. I lifted her up, and petted her, and coaxed her, but it was no good; the only sign of life remaining was a drip of bright red blood.

Of course, I knew who had done it. There was but one man on earth, or under it, where the Devil dwells, who could have done such a thing. I used no harsher word about it, while I leaped upon our best horse, and set the head of Kickums towards the course now pointed out to me. Who showed me the course, I cannot tell. I only know that I took it. And the men fell back before me.

Weapon of no sort had I. Unarmed and wondering at my strange attire (with a bridal vest, wrought by our Annie, and red with the blood of the bride), I went forth just to find out this; whether in this world there be, or be not, God of Justice.

With my vicious horse at a furious speed, I came upon Black Barrow Down, directed by some shout of men, which seemed to me but a whisper. And there, about a furlong before me, rode a man on a great black horse; and I knew the man was Carver Doone.

" Thy life, or mine," I said to myself, " as the will of God may be. But we two live not upon this earth, one more hour, together."

Sometimes seeing no ground beneath me, and sometimes heeding every leaf and the crossing of the grass blades, I followed over the long moor, reckless whether seen or not. But only once the other man turned round and looked back again; and then I was beside a rock, with a reedy swamp behind me.

Although he was so far before me, and riding as hard as ride he might, I saw that he had something on the horse in front of him, something which needed care and stopped him from looking backward.

The man turned up the gully leading from the moor to Cloven Rocks, through which John Fry had tracked Uncle Ben, as of old related. But as Carver entered it, he turned round and beheld me not a hundred yards behind; and I saw that he was bearing his child, little Ensie, before him. Ensie also descried me, and stretched his hands, and cried to me; for the face of his father frightened him.

I followed my enemy carefully, steadily, even leisurely; for I had him, as in a pitfall, whence no escape might be. Now there is a way between cliff and slough, for those who know the ground thoroughly, or have time enough to search for it; but for him there was no road, and he lost some time in seeking it. Upon this, he made up his mind; and wheeling, fired, and then rode at me.

His bullet struck me somewhere, but I took no heed of that. Fearing only his escape, I laid my horse across the way, and with the limb of the oak, torn from a tree as I rode past, struck full on the forehead his charging steed. Ere the slash of the sword came nigh me, man and horse rolled over, and well-nigh bore my own horse down, with the power of their onset.

Carver was somewhat stunned, and could not arise for a moment. Meanwhile, I leaped on the ground and waited, smoothing my hair back and baring my arms, as though in a ring for wrestling. Then the little boy ran to me, clasped my leg and looked up at me, and the terror in his eyes made me almost fear myself.

" Ensie, dear," I said quite gently, grieving that he should see his wicked father killed, " run up yonder round the corner, and try to find a bunch of bluebells for the pretty lady."

With a sullen and black scowl, the Carver gathered his mighty limbs and arose and looked round for his weapons; but I had put them well away. Then he came to me and gazed, being wont to frighten thus young men.

" I would not harm you, lad," he said, with a lofty style of sneering. " I have punished you enough for most of your impertinence. For the rest I forgive you, because you have been good and gracious to my little son. Go, and be contented."

For answer, I smote him on the cheek, lightly, and not to hurt him, but to make his blood leap up. I would not sully my tongue by speaking to a man like this.

There was a level space of sward between us and the slough. With the courtesy derived from London and the processions I had seen, to this place I led him. And that he might breathe himself, and have every fibre cool and every muscle ready, my hold upon his coat I loosed; and left him to begin with me, whenever he thought proper.

I think that he felt that his time was come. I think he knew from my knitted muscles, and the firm arch of my breast, and the way in which I stood; but most of all from my stern blue eyes, that he had found his master. At any rate a paleness came, an ashy paleness on his cheeks, and the vast calves of his legs bowed in, as if he were out of training. We fought, and beneath the iron of my strength—for God that day was with me—I had him helpless in two minutes, and his blazing eyes lolled out.

" I will not harm thee any more," I cried, so far as I could for panting, the work being very furious: " Carver Doone, thou art beaten: own it, and thank God for it; and go thy way and repent thyself."

It was all too late. The black bog had him by the feet, and scarcely could I turn away, while he sank from sight.

When the little boy came back with the bluebells, I heavily mounted my horse again and looked down at the innocent Ensie.

" Don "—for he never could say " John "—" oh, Don, I am so glad, that nasty naughty man is gone away. Take me home, Don. Take me home."

It hurt me more than I can tell even through all other grief, to take into my arms the child of the man just slain by me. But I could not leave him there till someone else might fetch him, on account of the cruel slough, and the ravens which had come hovering over the dead horse.

I had spent a great deal of blood and was rather faint and weary. And it was lucky for me that Kickums had lost spirit, like his master, and went home as mildly as a lamb. Only the thought of Lorna's death, like a heavy knell, was tolling in the belfry of my brain.

When we came to the stable door, I rather fell from my horse than got off.

" I have killed him," was all I said, " even as he killed Lorna. Now let me see my wife, mother. She belongs to me none the less, though dead."

" You cannot see her now, dear John," said Ruth Huckaback, coming forward, since no one else had the courage. " Annie is with her now, John."

" What has that to do with it ? Let me see my dead one, and then die."

Ruth alone stood by me, and dropped her eyes and trembled.

" John, she is not your dead one. She may even be your living one yet, your wife, your home, and your happiness. But you must not see her now."

" Is there any chance for her ? For me, I mean; for me, I mean ? "

" God in heaven knows, dear John. But the sight of you, and in this sad plight, would be certain death to her. Now come first, and be healed yourself."

I obeyed her like a child, whispering only as I went, for

none but myself knew her goodness: " Almighty God will bless you, darling, for the good you are doing now."

If it had not been for this little maid, Lorna must have died at once, as in my arms she lay for dead, from the dastard and murderous cruelty. But the moment I left her Ruth came forward and took the command of everyone, in right of her firmness and readiness.

She made them bear her home at once upon the door of the pulpit with the cushion under the drooping head. With her own little hands she cut off, as tenderly as a pear is peeled, the bridal dress, probed the vile wound in the side, and fetched the reeking bullet forth; and then with the coldest water staunched the flowing of the life-blood. She opened Lorna's lips and poured wine into her mouth.

For hours, however, and days, she lay at the very verge of death, kept alive by nothing but the care, the skill, the tenderness, and perpetual watchfulness of Ruth. But my broken rib, which was set by a doctor, who chanced to be at the wedding, was allotted to Annie's care; and great inflammation ensuing, it was quite enough to content her. This doctor had pronounced poor Lorna dead; wherefore Ruth refused most firmly to have aught to do with him. She took the whole case on herself; and with God's help she bore it through.

Now whether it were the light and brightness of my Lorna's nature, or the freedom from anxiety, Lorna recovered long ere I did. For a long time I lay there with the doctor coming to bleed me regularly. One day, when I was expecting him, a little knock sounded through my gloomy room, and supposing it to be the doctor, I tried to rise and make my bow. But to my surprise, it was little Ruth, who had never once come to visit me, since I was placed under the doctor's hands. Ruth was dressed so gaily, with rosettes, and flowers and what not, that I was sorry for her bad manners; and thought she was come to conquer me, now that Lorna was done with.

Ruth ran towards me with sparkling eyes, being rather

short of sight; then suddenly she stopped, and I saw entire amazement in her face.

" Can you receive visitors, Cousin Ridd—why, they never told me of this! " she cried. " I knew that were you weak, dear John, but not that you were dying. Whatever is that basin for ?"

" I have no intention of dying, Ruth, and I like not to talk about it. But that basin, if you must know, is for the doctor's purpose."

"What, do you mean bleeding you? You poor weak cousin! Is it possible that he does that still?"

" Twice a week for the last six weeks, dear. Nothing else has kept me alive."

" Nothing else has killed you, nearly. There! " and she set her little boot across the basin and crushed it. " Not another drop shall they have from you."

I was surprised to see Ruth excited, her character being so calm and quiet. And I tried to soothe her with my feeble hand, as now she knelt before me.

" Dear cousin, the doctor must know best. Annie says so every day. Else what has he been brought up for ? "

" Brought up for slaying and murdering. Twenty doctors killed King Charles in spite of all the women. Will you leave it to me, John ? I have saved your Lorna's life. And now I will save yours; which is a far, far easier business."

" You have saved my Lorna's life ? What do you mean by talking so ? "

" Only what I say, Cousin John. Though I over-prize my work. But at any rate she says so."

" I do not understand," I said, falling back with bewilderment; " all women are such liars."

" Have you ever known me to tell a lie ? " cried Ruth in great indignation—more feigned I doubt, than real. " Your mother may tell a story now and then, when she feels it right; and so may both your sisters. But so you cannot do, John Ridd; and no more than you, can I do it."

" I do not understand " was all I could say, for a very long time.

"Will you understand if I show you Lorna? I have feared to do it for the sake of you both. But now Lorna is well enough, if you think you are, cousin John. Surely you will understand, when you see your wife."

Before I had time to listen much for the approach of footsteps, Ruth came back, and behind her Lorna. Ruth banged the door and ran away; and Lorna stood before me.

But she did not stand for an instant when she saw what I was like. At the risk of all thick bandages, and upsetting a dozen medicine bottles, and scattering leeches right and left, she managed to get into my arms, although they could not hold her. She laid her panting warm young breast on the place where they meant to bleed me, and she set my pale face up; and she would not look at me, having greater faith in kissing.

I felt my life come back and glow; I felt my trust in God revive. I felt the joy of living and loving dearer things than life. It is not a moment to describe; who feels can never tell of it. But the compassion of my sweetheart's tears, and the caressing of my bride's lips, and the throbbing of my wife's heart (now at last at home on mine), made me feel that the world was good, and not a thing to be weary of.

Little more have I to tell. The doctor was turned out at once; and slowly came back my former strength, with a darling wife and good victuals. As for Lorna, she never tired of sitting and watching me eat and eat. And such is her heart, that she never tires of being with me here and there, among the beautiful places, and talking with her arm around me—so far at least, as it can go, though half of mine may go round her—of the many fears and troubles, dangers and discouragements, and worst of all the bitter partings, which we used to undergo.

There is no need for my farming harder than becomes a man of weight. Lorna has great stores of money, though we never draw it out, except for some poor neighbour; unless I find her a sumptuous dress, out of her own perquisites.

As for poor Tom Faggus, everyone knows his bitter

adventures, when his pardon was recalled because of his sally to Sedgemoor. But he eluded his captors until a new king arose. Upon this Tom sued his pardon afresh; and Jeremy Stickles, who suited the times, was glad to help him in getting it, as well as a compensation. Thereafter, the good and respectable Tom lived a godly and righteous (though not always sober) life; and brought up his children to honesty, as the first of all qualifications.

My dear mother was as happy as possibly need be with us; having no cause for jealousy, as others arose around her. And everybody was well pleased when Lizzie came in one day and tossed her bookshelf over, and declared that she would have Captain Bloxham, and nobody should prevent her; for that he alone, of all the men she had ever met, knew good writing when he saw it, and could spell a word when told. As he had now succeeded to Captain Stickles' position (Stickles going up the tree), and had the power of collecting and of keeping what he liked, there was nothing to be said against it, and we hoped that he would pay her out.

I sent little Ensie to Blundell's school, at my own cost and charges, having changed his name for fear of what anyone might do to him. I called him " Ensie Jones ", and I hope that he will be a credit to us. For the bold adventurous nature of the Doones broke out on him, and we got him a commission, and after many scrapes of spirit he did great things in the Low Countries. He looks upon me as his father; and without my leave will not lay claim to the heritage and title of the Doones which clearly belong to him.

Ruth Huckaback is not married yet, although upon Uncle Reuben's death she came into all his property; except indeed, two thousand pounds, which Uncle Ben, in his driest manner, bequeathed to " Sir John Ridd, the worshipful knight, for greasing of the testator's boots ". And he left almost a mint of money, not from the mine, but from the shop and the good use of usury. For the mine had brought in just what it cost, when the vein of gold ended suddenly; leaving all concerned much older, and some, I fear, much poorer, but no one utterly ruined, as is the case with most of them. Ruth herself was his true mine, as upon death-bed he found. I know a man even worthy of her: and though she is not very young, he loves her as I love Lorna. More and more, I hope and think that in the end he will win her; and I do not mean to dance again, except at dear Ruth's wedding; if a floor can be found strong enough.

Of Lorna, of my lifelong darling, of my more and more loved wife, I will not talk; for it is not seemly that a man should exalt his pride. Year by year her beauty grows, with the growth of goodness, kindness, and true happiness—above all with loving. For change she makes a joke of this, and plays with it, and laughs at it; and then, when my slow nature marvels, back she comes to the earnest thing. And if I wish to pay her out for something very dreadful—as may happen once or twice when we become too gladsome—I bring her to forgotten sadness, and to me for cure of it, by the two words, " Lorna Doone ".